EMERGENCY NURSE

Nurse Marion Talbot and Doctor Alan Vincent work together in Casualty. Marion is drawn to him a little more every day — but wonders what she can do to attract his attention. Then they each reveal they will have a relative visiting soon: Marion her mother, and Alan his uncle; and so they hatch a plan to give them a good time, while deciding to meet up themselves. But when a nurse from the hospital is attacked, and the police become involved, things do not run as smoothly as they had anticipated . . .

PHYLLIS MALLET

EMERGENCY NURSE

Complete and Unabridged

LINFORD
Leicester

First published in Great Britain in 1968

First Linford Edition
published 2018

A catalogue record for this book is available
from the British Library.

ISBN 978–1–4448–3875–6

Published by
F. A. Thorpe (Publishing)
Anstey, Leicestershire

Set by Words & Graphics Ltd.
Anstey, Leicestershire
Printed and bound in Great Britain by
T. J. International Ltd., Padstow, Cornwall

This book is printed on acid-free paper

1

The evening was foggy, and Marion Talbot suppressed a little sigh as she walked in through the big main doors of Regent's General Hospital and made her way along the brightly lit corridors to the Casualty Department. The weather governed the degree of work which might come into the department during the night, and fog was worse than anything. They could expect a spate of accident cases before the night was over, for the large city of Ambury, in Suffolk and close to the Essex border, had an average accident rate.

As she reached the big double doors at the end of the corridor, Marion paused to glance into a small office on the right, and an ambulance driver looked up at her and grinned in friendly fashion.

'You'll be going out with us tonight, Nurse?' he demanded.

1

'If there are any emergency calls,' Marion replied, and smiled when he shook his head in wonder.

'I've never seen an optimist like you,' he declared. 'Of course there will be calls in weather like this. We've been out twice in the past hour.'

'So they're pretty busy in there!' Marion nodded towards the glass door, and her eyes took in the large black lettering marked on one of them. 'Casualty Department', she read, and a thrill spasmed through her breast. She was thinking of Alan Vincent, who would be inside. As Casualty Officer, he had been on duty every evening this week, and although Marion had seen quite a lot of him in that time, he hadn't appeared any friendlier. She was beginning to think that what the other nurses said about him was true. He was just plain anti-social!

She turned away from the little office and pushed open one of the big doors, passing into the department, and again she paused, this time glancing at the dozen or so people seated on the rows of chairs; some waiting to see the Casualty Officer, and some being the relatives or friends who had accompanied them. There was a trolley by the far door, on which lay an accident case waiting to be wheeled to the nearby X-ray department, and a nurse appeared from an open doorway on the left and bent to examine the patient.

Marion went forward to the little staff office, and found Staff-nurse Jannis glancing at her watch. They smiled at each other, both anxious. Marion wanted to get on duty and start working and the staff-nurse wanted to get away after a busy term. The Casualty and Admission Centre was the scene of great activity both day and night, and sometimes it was hard to tell the time of day. It was a busy department, and although the nurses were thoroughly tired at the end of their duty, the incessant running around made the time seem to pass more quickly.

'You're in for a busy evening,' the staff-nurse commented, giving Marion details of the patients awaiting treatment, and she handed over the keys to the drugs cupboard. 'But I'm off now. I hope you don't get called out too many times during the night.'

Marion nodded soberly. Ambulance duty was a departure from the old ways of handling traffic accidents and other serious cases. Instead of an ambulance travelling to the scene of the incident to pick up victims to take them to the hospital, where skilled aid awaited, a doctor and a nurse went out with the ambulance in order to start treatment immediately, and this valuable saving of time had proved greatly successful in the short time the scheme had been in operation. Sometimes minutes were vital to a badly injured patient, and already many accident victims were living now solely because skilled treatment had been available whilst the ambulance was travelling to the hospital.

When the Staff-nurse had gone Marion went to give some instructions to the two junior nurses in the department, then went on a quick tour to take in all that was happening. She went into the Consulting-room to see if the doctor needed any help.

Her heart seemed to skip a beat when she paused in the doorway to look at Alan Vincent. He was tall and slim, aged about twenty-six, and his blue eyes glanced up at her, seeming to narrow a little as they took in her trim figure.

'Good evening, Nurse,' he greeted her curtly, and Marion tightened her lips. There seemed no way of thawing him out, she thought. He was remote, aware only of the stream of patients coming before him, and she wished there was a possibility of breaking down his reserve and really getting to know him. In the past six months he had not taken out a single girl, according to the gossip that went the rounds, and the nurses were keenly interested in all his movements.

'Good evening, Doctor Vincent,' she replied with a little smile, and turned her attention to the patient seated on the chair beside the desk. The doctor was examining one of the man's eyes, and Marion waited quietly in the background.

'Yes,' Alan Vincent commented gently. 'I think we've managed to get it all out, Mr Jones. I suggest in future that you do wear those protective glasses your employers provide. Your sight is very precious, you know.'

'Yes, Doctor, I realize that now,' the man replied. 'I shan't be such a fool again.'

Marion watched keenly, liking Alan Vincent's sympathetic manner towards the patients. He had a very nice way about him, and nothing was too much trouble for him. He always worked tirelessly, and gave consideration to the nurses with whom he worked, but that was as far as he went, and Marion told herself, as she watched him, that each passing day was finding her a little more attracted to him.

There was a tap at the door as the patient got to his feet, and Marion opened it quietly, to confront one of the juniors.

'Please, Nurse, there's a telephone call for you.'

'For me?' Marion frowned, her forehead wrinkling, her dark eyes glinting. It could only be her mother, she thought swiftly, and stepped back as the patient left the room. 'Thank you, Nurse, I shan't be a moment.' She glanced at Alan Vincent, and found that he was staring at her. 'Would you excuse me for a moment, Doctor? It must be important. I don't let anyone call me when I'm on duty.'

'Of course, Nurse,' he replied with a little smile. 'I wish all the nurses were as considerate as you.'

'It must be my mother,' she said. 'She lives alone in York, and I know from her letters that she hasn't been feeling too well lately.'

Turning on her heel, Marion left the office and went along to the staff room. The telephone receiver lay on the desk, and Marion closed the door and sat down, taking up the receiver with fingers that trembled a little.

'Hello, this is Nurse Talbot.'

'Marion, dear, you do sound stern. Is anything wrong?'

'Mother! I guessed it was you, and I was worried. I thought something was wrong. You don't usually call me. Are you all right? You never let me know if you are ill, but I've been reading between the lines of your letters. How are you keeping?'

'Not too badly, dear! As a matter of fact I have been ill, although not seriously, and I didn't want to alarm you so I kept it to myself. But I'm all right again now. Doctor Lamb has been keeping a strict eye on me. He's told me to take a little holiday. I protested, of course, it being so near Christmas, but he was firm, so I've decided to come visit you for a few days. Will you be able to get some time off?'

'I'm due a long weekend,' Marion said cheerfully. 'It will be lovely to see you again. The weeks seem to fly by, don't they? When are you coming?'

'Whenever you think I should, dear.' There was an anxious note in Jessica Talbot's voice. 'I don't want to upset any previous arrangements that you might have made.'

'Mother, you know perfectly well that I don't have male friends,' Marion said with a smile. She thought of Alan Vincent as she spoke, and told herself that there was one man she would like to know more about. 'I don't make arrangements for future dates. I'm usually too busy here at the hospital to worry about things like that.'

'Then there must be something wrong with you. You're twenty-three, and if you don't soon start looking around for a prospective husband you're going to finish up on the shelf, my girl.' There was a half-mocking note in Mrs Talbot's tones now, and Marion smiled.

'Well we'll discuss that when you arrive. Have you thought about where you'll be staying?'

'I thought I'd leave that to you. Pick me a small hotel somewhere close to the hospital. I think you did mention at sometime or other that there was such a place where people visiting the hospital staff usually stay. Don't they cater specially for such people?'

'Yes. You're talking about the Regent Hotel.' Marion laughed, and she glanced quickly over her shoulder as she heard the door opening at her back. She caught her breath as Alan Vincent peered in. 'Everything is Regency around this district. The hospital is called Regent's, because it's standing in Regent Road. The hotel has the same name, and at the far end of the street there's the Regent Cinema. But just a moment, mother, I may be wanted.' She lowered the receiver and glanced at Alan Vincent, who was standing in the doorway.

'It's all right, Nurse,' he said. 'I was just wondering if there was an emergency for you. Is everything all right?'

'Yes thank you, Doctor!' She was surprised by his concern. 'It is my mother, but she's recovering from an illness which she had kept secret, and she's planning to come and spend a few days here in Ambury with me. I was just telling her that I thought it would be all right if she stayed at the Regent Hotel.'

'I can recommend it,' he said with a faint smile. 'It's where my uncle stays when he comes to visit me. As a matter of fact he's coming down this weekend. But I'll let you get on with your call.' He stepped out of the room and closed the door, and Marion lifted the receiver again.

'Hello, Mother,' she called. 'It's all right. I have a little more time. I'll book a room for you at the Regent Hotel. Now when will you be arriving?'

'Friday evening,' came the prompt reply. 'Will you be on duty?'

'No. As it's my long weekend, I shall be finishing when I come off duty on Friday morning. I had planned to come home this weekend to see you, but it will be lovely to have you here, and it will make such a nice change for you. The weather isn't too bad right now, although it's foggy this evening, but we'll be able to get around. Will you leave me to make all the arrangements? When you arrive at the railway station get a taxi to take you to the Regent Hotel, and everything will be ready for you. I'd better go now, because we're very busy.'

'Yes, dear. I shall look forward to seeing you on Friday evening. Goodbye for now.'

'Goodbye, Mother.' Marion hung up slowly, and there was a smile on her face as she got to her feet and left the office. Her mother lived a lonely life, and several times Marion had tried to induce her to give up her home in York and take a flat here in Ambury, but Mrs Talbot clung to the things of the past. Marion's father, a doctor, had died years before, and since that tragedy there had been nothing worthwhile in Jessica Talbot's life, except her daughter. But with Marion now a qualified nurse and living away from home there seemed to be nothing for Jessica Talbot to do with her life. She did belong to a club, and was some sort of an official in a Women's Institute, but she had no lasting interests, and Marion had been worried for some time about her mother.

She was frowning as she left the office, and Alan Vincent was waiting for her. She paused in surprise, watching his slow smile with interested attention. He had never appeared so human before.

'Everything all right?' he demanded, and smiled again as she nodded. 'I know how it is when you're living away from home. I'm in the same position. I lived with my uncle and aunt for years, after my parents were killed in a car accident, but my aunt died three years ago, and since then Uncle Jim has been a source of worry to me. I've tried to get him to sell up in London and move to Ambury, but he's reluctant to tear up roots.'

'That's exactly what I've been trying to do with my mother!' Marion allowed surprise to edge her tones. 'I haven't been too successful either.' She laughed. 'Our problems are similar. If you do manage to find a solution you might let me know about it.'

'I'll do that.' He was smiling as he moved away. 'I shall be in the end cubicle if you need me. A man was found unconscious in the street. Come along there in a moment, will you?'

Marion nodded, and as she went along to the treatment room she buried her personal thoughts away in the back of her mind. But she could not stifle the thrill that wandered through her. Alan Vincent had actually forgotten that they were on duty, and had spoken to her as if she were a human being and not just a nurse on duty to help him.

The clang of an ambulance bell outside alerted her, and after glancing into the treatment room to see what the juniors were doing, Marion went to meet the stretcher that was being pushed in by the porter. An ambulance man came in, giving her details of the road accident that had occured and the first aid treatment which he had carried out. Marion saw to it that the patient was wheeled into a cubicle, and she drew the green curtains as she entered to examine the slim body of the teenage girl lying on the trolley.

The girl's eyes flickered open, wide and staring, filled with pain and fear, and Marion spoke soothingly as she smoothed back dark hair from a muddy forehead.

'Don't worry, dear, and lie perfectly still,' she said. 'You'll be all right. Can you tell me where you hurt?'

'My legs,' came the faint reply. 'It was my fault. I was running across the road, and I never saw the car. I should have been more careful, what with the fog and all.'

'The doctor will be along to see you shortly. Just lie nice and quiet. Are you in much pain?'

'Not at the moment. I'm worried about my mother. She'll be expecting me home. I was working late this evening.'

'There'll be a policeman here shortly

to ask you about the accident, and he'll go to your home and tell your parents.'

'I haven't got a father,' the girl said, and she closed her eyes and a tear squeezed itself from under an eyelid. 'He died last year. My mother will be all alone now. I shall have to stay in here, won't I? I think my legs are broken.'

'You'll be all right,' Marion whispered. 'What is your name, and where do you live?'

The girl told her, and Marion wrote down the details. She patted the girl's shoulder and quickly left the cubicle, calling one of the juniors to go in and stay with the girl. Then she went along to the end cubicle, where Alan Vincent was just completing an examination of the man brought in unconscious from the street.

'There's a girl about sixteen in the second cubicle, Doctor Vincent,' Marion reported. 'Car accident . . . suspected fracture of both legs.'

Alan Vincent tut-tutted. 'This is going to be a night of nights,' he commented.

'I'm expecting the bell to go for an emergency. I don't know why, but I've got a presentiment. You'll be ready to leave at a moment's notice, won't you?'

'Yes, Doctor.'

'Good. Ring Men's Medical and tell them we're sending a patient up, will you. Suspected insulin overdose. The patient is a diabetic. Here's his card with all the details. I'll have a word with Doctor Howard when you can raise him on the phone. Get the porter to bring in the trolley. This man must have immediate treatment.' He paused, taking the card from Marion's hand which bore the details of the girl involved in the accident. 'I'll be in the second cubicle if you should want me.'

'I'll be along there as soon as I can,' Marion promised, and was aware that he stared at her as she hurried away to the telephone.

The evening passed quickly, and there seemed to be no slowing of the incidents that occurred. Marion was running around incessantly, handling

17

first one problem and then another, and she had long since ceased to be astonished by the variety of cases that came in to them . . . a man slipped off a slowly moving bus and fractured his skull, a boy ran into a lamp post on his bicycle and cut his forehead so badly it needed four stitches, a girl caught her fingers in a slamming car door! So it went on, and it was some hours before there was a slight relaxing of the high note of action. But just after eleven there seemed to be a pause, and Marion went along to the Consulting-room to find Alan Vincent seated at the desk, trying to catch up on his many reports. He looked up with a smile as she peered around the door at him.

'You're looking tired, Nurse,' he remarked, and Marion smiled. 'What have you got for me?'

'Nothing at the moment,' Marion replied, smiling. 'I thought you'd like some coffee now.'

'It would go down very well,' he assured her with gratitude. 'It's been a busy evening, hasn't it.'

'I've never known it to be any different in this department,' she replied. 'It's amazing the number of people who have accidents in this city. It makes one wonder what the percentage is for going through life without incident.'

'Accidents are one of the prices we pay for civilization,' he said somewhat forlornly. 'Personally I wish the motor car had never been invented.'

'Your parents!' Marion said involuntarily, and stopped herself from saying more. She took a deep breath and started backing out of the doorway. 'I'll hurry up the coffee,' she said, and closed the door with a sigh. For a moment she stood motionless in the corridor, and then she shook her dark head and went towards the little kitchen, which was beyond the small operating theatre.

One of the juniors appeared from the theatre, and she looked flushed and worried. Marion paused quickly.

'Anything wrong, Nurse?' she demanded. Before the nurse could reply there was a movement in the theatre doorway, and Martin Salmon, the porter, appeared and edged around them both. He looked a trifle sheepish, Marion thought, and recalled that Salmon, a man of thirty, handsome and aware of it, had been courting this Junior for some time.

'Nothing is wrong, Nurse,' came the reply, and Marion nodded.

'All right,' she said. 'But don't get caught, Nurse.'

She went on her way, thinking of Alan Vincent. He was human behind that wall of his, she told herself, and wondered how she could get through his reserve. There must be a way of reaching him. There had to be some common ground between them.

With the coffee made, Marion forestalled one of the Juniors and took Alan Vincent's along to the Consulting-room, tapping at the door with a definite thrill running through her. She opened the door at his command and went in, waiting for him to look up at her, and he smiled as he did so.

'You're a welcome sight,' he commented, taking the cup and saucer from her, and Marion took a deep breath as their hands touched briefly. 'Are you in a hurry now, Nurse?'

'No,' Marion replied. 'Things have quietened down for a spell. These lulls are very necessary for us to get everything up to date. The theatre is clean again and ready for use.'

She watched him closely, watching the shadows playing on his face as he bent his head forward to glance at his pile of reports. His fair hair was long and wavy, and she had to resist the impulse to reach out and stroke it. She smiled as she mastered the impish urge and turned to leave.

'Don't go, unless your own coffee is waiting for you. I'd like to talk to you if I may.'

'Certainly.' She halted and stared at him, becoming aware of the silence in the room, the tension that mounted swiftly as she waited for his words. His face showed that he was instantly under a considerable strain, and she wondered at it. Then he shook his head.

'It doesn't matter, Nurse,' he said quickly. 'Go and get your coffee before it gets cold. We may be rushing off out before we know where we are. Have you checked that the people who are supposed to cover for us while we're out are standing by?'

'That was one of the first things I did when I came on duty,' she said with a smile.

He nodded, smiling faintly. 'You're very efficient, Nurse,' he said heavily, and added almost inaudibly, 'too damned efficient.'

Marion stared at him, almost disbelieving her ears.

'I beg your pardon, Doctor!' she said.

He was not smiling now, and there was a slight flush in his cheeks as he stared at her. His face was expressionless, his lips compressed, and Marion felt a tremor in her breast as she awaited his next words.

'You're not like a human girl,' he

said. 'Everything is always under control with you. You're so cool and efficient, like a machine. I'm only a poor male, and I'm scared half to death to ask you out for fear of a refusal. You don't seem to concern yourself with men. I've never known you to see one in an evening. You're in love with your work, and there's nothing else in the world for you. If that's the way you feel why the devil did Nature make you so beautiful?'

Marion stared at him non-plussed, not knowing how to answer. Her face was flushing. She could feel the heat in her cheeks. He got up from his seat, putting down his coffee, and came around the desk to confront her. She stared up into his face, wondering if perhaps this was not some dream that had been sent to torment her.

'Would you consider going out with me, Nurse Talbot?' he demanded. 'I'm feeling terribly lonely, and I must have some company before I turn neurotic. All work and no play is a bad thing, especially in this business.' He held up a hand as Marion opened her mouth to reply. 'Don't stop me now I've got started,' he commanded curtly. 'I've been a long time plucking up the courage to ask. It hasn't been for the nerve to ask you but for fear that having got it out, you might say no. I don't know what you've got against men, but I'm a plain, straight-forward, simple person, and I'd like your company for an evening.'

'I've got nothing against men, gener-ally,' Marion replied slowly. 'Perhaps I never go out with them because I rarely get asked by anyone. I do have some-thing of a reputation for saying no, but that was because the wrong men asked me in the first place. But you're not one of the wrong men, Doctor Vincent, and if you would like me to go out on a date then I'll do so.'

His face showed surprise, and Marion shook her head as she smiled. But before he could reply the alarm bell rang briefly, warning them that the emergency ambu-lance was being called out. Everything was forgotten from that moment onwards, and Marion rushed to ring for their stand-by while Alan Vincent grabbed up what he needed to take with him and hurried out of the department, calling for Marion to hurry . . .

2

Marion was breathless as she climbed into the ambulance, and the vehicle lurched forward, gathering speed quickly as it sped away on its errand of mercy. Alan Vincent sat opposite Marion; they were in the back of the ambulance, and he had taken off his white coat and pulled on a jacket. His fair head was bent over one of the black leather bags as he checked the contents, and Marion watched him closely. She was wondering where they were going and what had happened, and she turned her head and peered out through a window, surprised to see that the fog had lifted considerably. Visibility was almost normal, she supposed, and that would account for the lessening of incidents which had occurred earlier. When she glanced back at Alan Vincent he was studying her face, and he smiled as their eyes met.

'You must think I'm an idiot,' he ventured. 'I feel like one now. Fancy talking to you like that! I'll bet you've never had anyone ask for a date in such a round-about way, have you?'

'It was unusual,' Marion replied.

'And did you answer it?' he demanded. 'That call came through so fast I missed anything you said.'

'I told you I'd be delighted to go out with you, Doctor.'

'Good. I was hoping against hope that you would say yes.' He was at ease now, and his smile was natural. 'We'll have time later to fix the details, won't we?'

'We can always make time,' she asserted. 'Did the driver tell you where we're going?'

'Yes. There's been an accident at a factory. A lift collapsed, taking four men down three floors. It will be a nasty mess, by all accounts.'

Marion sighed. There was always something happening to people! Not a minute went by through all the ages without someone happening with a mishap some-where in the world. But one good thing about civilization, she thought, was that medical knowledge had increased, and so had surgical practice. She glanced around the specially equipped interior of the ambulance, and nodded slowly. This was indeed a vehicle of mercy!

The ambulance eventually slowed down, and then came to a halt. The doors were opened, and as they alighted, Marion saw that they were standing in a factory yard. Several men were in view, and one of them came hurrying forward.

'This way,' he gasped. 'We've man-aged to get them out of the shaft. They're lying on blankets in the basement.'

Alan Vincent followed quickly, with Marion trying to keep up with them. The ambulance driver and his mate came along behind with a stretcher. They de-scended a flight of stone steps into a large basement, and there was a little group of watching men standing around four prone figures lying on the ground. The men stepped back as Vincent hurried across, and one of them pointed to one of the four figures.

'He's more seriously hurt than the other three, Doctor.'

Alan nodded and approached the figure, dropping to one knee, setting down the bag he carried, and Marion went to one of the others, acting coolly and confidently. These men had crashed from a great height, and they would be badly shocked, apart from any injuries they had sustained. She found the man bleeding badly from a head wound, and took the man's pulse. Moving on to the next, she bent quickly, and the man's eyes flickered open for a moment.

'It's my back, Nurse,' he muttered, before closing his eyes again and lapsing into unconsciousness.

Marion turned to go to Alan's side, and found him working swiftly to staunch the bleeding that was coming from his patient's head. He glanced at Marion momentarily, his face set in grim lines. 'Broken leg here as well,' he said, and she waited for the ambulance men to

29

arrive, taking the splints from one of them.

Within minutes the four men had been attended to, and there was no lack of help to carry them up to the ambulance, where they were quickly but gently set to rest. Alan was still working on the more seriously injured man as the vehicle sped back to the hospital.

An hour passed before all four men had been treated, and by the time they had been sent up to the wards, Marion was feeling the effects of the tension. She had a headache nagging inside, and went to her little office for some aspirin. As she sat for a moment to relax she let her mind open to her personal thoughts, and she smiled as she pictured Alan Vincent's face. So he had wanted to ask her out before, but lacked the nerve! That was a revelation! She thought critically about that. She had a reputation for not going out. She was labelled anti-social. But that was not the way of it. She didn't feel that way. She just didn't know the answer to the situation into which she seemed to have fallen. She didn't dislike men. It was just that she never met the right ones, and that was exactly what she had told Alan.

But he was the right one. She sensed that, and it did something to her inside. There was a little knot of emotion swelling in her breast. The knowledge that he was attracted to her was a shock, and it was at work upon her romantic self. She was lonely for romance. That much she had been aware of for a long time, but no man at the hospital had appealed to her, except Alan, and it seemed too good to be true that he should suddenly begin to show some interest in her.

There was a tap at the door, and she got wearily to her feet as the door opened. Alan walked in, smiling. Already there seemed to be a great difference about him. For months she had watched him working behind that shield of reserve that was in him, but now it was gone, apparently shattered by the revelation he had made. Would that make him vulnerable to romance? Marion didn't know, but she was telling herself that she would make no mistake with him. She wouldn't try to rush him or try to take the initiative. It would have to be left up to him, but if he did need a helping hand then she would be ready to see it, and she would lead him along. She pulled herself from her thoughts, surprised that it was in her to plan ahead in such a manner. But he was different! The thought kept repeating itself in her mind.

'How are you feeling?' he demanded, leaving the door open and dropping into the chair beside the desk. He motioned for Marion to sit down again, which she did thankfully.

'I have a slight headache,' she replied. 'But it is nothing. I'm feeling excited.'

'About your mother coming here this weekend?' His blue eyes were bright and watchful.

'Among other things.'

'My Uncle Jim is supposed to be coming to see me any weekend now. He likes coming here, and visits quite frequently. I might ring him, this being only Wednesday, and ask him to come. Between us we might be able to give your mother and my uncle a good time this weekend.' There was a hopeful gleam in his eyes as he spoke, and Marion smiled.

'That sounds like a good idea,' she commented. 'I think my mother would appreciate a surprise like that. She used to like a social life, but these latter years have been very dull for her, especially after I took up nursing.'

'Very well.' He glanced at his wristwatch. 'First thing in the morning I'll ring Uncle Jim and tell him to come down. He stays at the Regent Hotel, so he won't be far away. When is your mother arriving?'

'On Friday evening. I have a long weekend this week. I go off duty on Friday morning and I'm finished until Monday morning.'

'Lucky you, but I have all day Sunday off. What can we do? The weather is all against picnics and that sort of thing. It may not even be pleasant to go for a drive.'

'Let's wait and see what kind of a day it is,' Marion suggested with a smile, and he nodded gravely. She could see that he was going to make an issue of making sure her mother and his uncle enjoyed themselves at the weekend, and from there he would go on to acquaint himself with her. She wondered what had started him off towards her? It had been weeks and weeks before he had even noticed her in the hospital, and the tales that went around about him almost convinced her that he was the shyest man on the staff. But he didn't seem the shy type. She couldn't imagine him being shy.

'I'm relieved that I've got my greatest problem off my chest,' he ventured slowly. 'I was afraid to ask you out,' he broke off. 'What's your first name, Marion isn't it?'

'That's right.' She nodded.

'And I'm Alan. Perhaps we had better restrict ourselves to Doctor and Nurse on duty, but there's no need for that when we're alone. You know something? I feel that I've known you for a long time.'

'Well, we've been working together for a good many months.'

'That isn't what I mean.' He studied her lovely face for a moment, and there seemed to be a wistfulness creeping into his expression. 'I'd like to know what makes you tick, Marion. What have you been looking for in a man that's made the right one so hard to find?'

'That isn't the way of it,' she replied, smiling in amusement. 'I haven't been looking at men with any object in mind. I'm wrapped up in my work here, and really, my world is very small. I haven't accustomed myself to looking around outside of it, and apart from you there's no one in the hospital I would care to go out with.'

'That's nice to know!' He was smiling broadly now, and he leaned forward peering into her face. 'You've got the most beautiful brown eyes I've ever seen,' he declared. 'And your hair is a wonderful chestnut. It looks like sullen gold.'

'That's a strange phrase,' she remarked. 'Sullen gold! I like it.' She paused. 'But tell me why you haven't been seeing any of the nurses. There's been keen competition between all the girls, and the first one to be taken out by you will be regarded as something of a heroine.'

'That will be you.' He was completely confident now. 'I hope you won't get your eyes scratched out by some jealous colleague.'

'I don't think they're as bad as that, but our going out together will cause a great deal of surprise and comment.' Marion took a suddenly realistic view of the situation, and she liked what she saw. Everyone would be saying what a dark horse she was, but she didn't mind that. He would probably have his leg pulled by the other doctors, and suddenly she thought of Ken Harland. He had been trying to get her to go out with him for almost as long as she'd been hoping that Alan would notice her. Harland was a colleague, and nice enough, but not Marion's type, and she hadn't wanted to hurt him. She had managed to turn him down so far, but of late he had become persistent, and her argument that she never went around with any man would soon dissolve. Then she wouldn't have any excuse at all.

But when he saw her going around with Alan he would probably get the message, and that would be all right. Marion liked everything to be tidy in her mind, and she didn't want any complication to spoil what seemed to be a promising start to a desired friendship with Alan. She studied his face as he got to his feet.

'I'd better get back and catch up on my reports,' he announced. 'We never know what's going to happen, and I'd hate to have to sit up in the morning and complete them. I'm getting impatient now, but we can't go out for an evening this week, can we? Why the devil didn't I ask you last week when we were both free in the evenings?'

He left her then, and Marion sat at the desk and considered the sudden change that had come about. It seemed too good to be true, but she could understand that he had slowly become more lonely with the passing months, until he could stand it no longer, and there was a tingle inside her as she thought of the evenings to come, when they would be able to go out together. She was looking forward to that. The winter wouldn't seen half so long with Alan Vincent around.

Going back to the treatment room, Marion found the two Juniors busy with their routine work, and she noticed that they were eyeing her curiously. She wondered if they had already seen the change of attitude between Alan and herself, and knew that rumours would spread very fast through the hospital. Such was the situation among the nurses that every so often a batch of rumours about Alan's new girl friend would be circulated, and days would pass before it was realized to be a false alarm. But this time there would be fire with the smoke, and Marion was happy that it would be her name linked with his.

The rest of the evening passed uneventfully, and when Alan went off to his quarters to get some sleep — he would be called if necessary, Marion had the Consulting-room cleaned and the entire department put into order for the day-staff. Then the small hours seemed to drag, and there was great silence in the department. With most of the lights switched off there was a ghostly atmosphere in the corridor and the small ante-rooms. There would be nothing doing, Marion knew from long experience, until traffic started getting around the streets again. She went back to the office to bring the book and cards up to date, and by the time the day-staff arrived she was feeling ready for bed.

She didn't see Alan again, and with

her duty over she went with the two Juniors to the nurses' dining room for a meal, but what she was really looking forward to was a shower. As she sat at one of the tables her friend, Rebecca Norris, came in from one of the wards. Tall and plump, with a generous face and kindly blue eyes, Rebbie Norris was something of a joker, and made life hectic in the nurses' home when she was off duty. She and Marion had taken to each other from the very first moment they met as student nurses, and had been together ever since. They were both twenty-three, and Rebbie was as fair as Marion was dark. They were similar in tastes, and went around together, neither having bothered with the opposite sex. Rebbie collected her breakfast and came and sat down beside Marion, sighing and leaning back in her seat for a moment, while her pale eyes regarded Marion's dark ones.

'My goodness!' Rebbie declared. 'I do believe I'm beginning to feel my age. It's all right for you young ones.' Her eyes sparkled with laughter as she glanced at the Juniors, who were smiling. 'Just wait till you get to my age. You won't be able to tread lightly into the dining room.'

'Poor old soul,' Marion commented. 'Matron was telling me only the other day that you were almost due to retire. She wondered what kind of a present you'd like.'

Rebbie smiled. She could never remain serious for very long, and her eyes showed a tell-tale glint as she regarded Marion. One of the Juniors giggled, and the other said, with uncertainty in her voice:

'Nurse Talbot has a very dark secret.'

Marion glanced at the younger nurses, and knew that they had noticed what had happened during the night.

'Nurse Talbot isn't the only one,' she replied severely. 'Who was being kissed by the porter in the theatre last night? You'd better not try that sort of thing when Sister West is on duty.'

The Junior in question went scarlet,

and Marion smiled But Rebbie Norris wouldn't be side-tracked.

'So Juniors are still doing all the things that generations of nurses have been doing,' she commented. 'But what's your dark secret, Marion? What's she been up to, girls?'

'Dr Vincent is Casualty Officer,' one of them replied.

'You don't mean — !' Rebbie broke off and stared at Marion with searching gaze. 'No,' she went on slowly. 'That's not possible. Alan Vincent isn't human. Nature made one of her rare mistakes with him. She made him with plenty of sex appeal, but forgot to put a spark of appreciation inside him. He doesn't know about girls, and that men should love them.'

'That's where you're wrong,' one of the Juniors persisted, evidently intent upon telling all she knew, and some of the night-staff at nearby tables were beginning to listen with attentive minds, for the name of Alan Vincent had been mentioned. 'I heard Dr

Vincent asking Nurse Talbot out for an evening.'

'What?' Rebbie stared at Marion, and other eyes came to rest upon her. 'Has he really fallen, Marion?'

'He did ask me out,' Marion admitted, knowing it would be better to get it out into the open for all to know rather than have a spate of rumours dragging the whole business out.

'You didn't turn him down, did you?' Rebbie asked anxiously. 'I know what you are, Marion, and if you rebuffed him he might go back into his shell forever. There are some of us around who would jump at the chance of a date with Alan Vincent.'

'I shall be seeing him on Sunday, I expect,' Marion admitted. She had finished her meal, and now she pushed back her chair and got to her feet. 'It's time to go to bed,' she said, her dark eyes sparkling as she surveyed the many interested faces turned towards her. 'But if you are all so interested in Alan Vincent then I'll tell you what he's like after I've been out with him.'

'I'll change places with you,' someone offered, and the others laughed.

'Not for anything,' Marion said. 'He's one man I'd change my way of life for.'

'Wait for me,' Rebbie Norris said, reaching out and grasping Marion's arm. 'I want to hear all about this date you've got yourself, and you'd better teach me your technique. If you're going to start seeing the doctors then I shall be left all on my own. We won't be going around together so very often, will we?'

'Don't be so silly,' Marion chided gently. 'I haven't even been out with him once yet. After the first time he may never want to see another woman as long as he lives.'

'Says you!' Rebbie was smiling. 'You'd better treat him very gently, Marion. If you do anything to spoil him for all the other nurses who'll be queueing to go out with him you'll be lynched. Now that he's started dating there may be no holding him. You'd better start putting in your orders, girls.'

Marion shook her head as she sat down again, and she waited for Rebbie to eat her breakfast. There was a lot of talk about Alan Vincent, all of it good-natured, and inside Marion there was a warm feeling that one of her dreams at least was about to come true.

When they left the dining room and started towards the nurses' home, which was built at the rear of the hospital and reached by way of narrow paths through extensive grounds, a voice called Marion's name, and she paused and turned to see Ken Harland hurrying towards her.

'Now you're in trouble,' Rebbie whispered as the doctor came up. 'You've got to put him off again. Shall I walk on? It's so embarrassing when he starts pleading to take you out.'

'No,' Marion replied fiercely. 'Wait for me, Rebbie, and don't be so hard on him. He's a very nice person.'

'But not up to your ideals, obviously.'

45

Rebbie lapsed into silence as Ken Harland arrived, and he was breathing heavily.

'Hello, Marion,' he greeted, not even looking at Rebbie Norris, who walked on a couple of paces and then paused. 'I've been looking around for you this morning.'

'What's on your mind, Ken?' Marion demanded, pulling her cape tightly around her. The morning was cold and windy, with splattering rain streaking around them. The sky was grey, seeming to bulge with rain clouds, and the early morning light was dull and bleak.

'I wondered what you'd be doing this weekend,' he said. 'I know you're off duty. I thought perhaps we could get together.' He fell silent and stared hopefully at her, and Marion took in his dark features and brown eyes. He was an attractive man, but there was nothing in him that caught at her dreams, and she was sorry for him.

'My mother is coming to Ambury for

the weekend,' she said. 'She hasn't been well lately, and her doctor prescribed a few days away from home.'

'Oh, well that's that.' His face showed disappointment, and Marion shook her head sympathetically, suppressing a sigh as she glanced around to see where Rebbie was.

'Ken, why don't you find yourself a nice girl?' she said involuntarily.

'You're about the nicest there is,' he said stoutly. 'What have you got against me, Marion?'

'Nothing, Ken, and you know it. I don't go around with anyone.'

'Then you don't know what you're missing,' he retorted. 'Why don't you give me a try? I'm not going to bite you when I get you alone.'

'I know that, Ken, but that's not the point. I don't want to go out with you, and it's nothing personal, mind you. You're just wasting your time over me. There must be lots of nurses here who'd like to go out with you.'

'I'm not interested in anyone else,' he

said doubtfully. 'Why don't you try it just once?'

'Let's talk about it some other time,' she suggested. 'I can't possibly see you this weekend.'

'All right. I am in rather a hurry this morning. I'll see you again. Sleep well. Was it a hectic night last night?'

'No worse than usual,' she admitted, and turned to catch up with Rebbie as he walked away.

'Well?' Rebbie demanded. 'Same old story?'

'Yes,' Marion replied slowly. 'I do feel sorry for him. He doesn't attract me in the least, and he's such a nice person.'

'Wait until he hears about you and Alan Vincent,' Rebbie said seriously. 'He's a strange character, Marion, and I mean that. He took out Nurse Reynolds once, and she swears that he's off-beat, and she was putting it kindly. You stick to Alan Vincent and you won't go far wrong.'

Marion was silent as they walked on to the home, and she thought deeply about the situation. She didn't want anyone or anything frightening off Alan now that he was showing some interest in her, and the fact that she had never given Ken Harland any encouragement wouldn't mean a thing if Alan thought she was seeing more than one man at a time. She stifled a yawn, ready to fall asleep, and she was almost too tired to take the shower she had promised herself. But she did, and Rebbie, who shared a room with her, felt constrained to do likewise. Then they went to their beds and prepared to sleep, and Marion's last conscious thought was of Alan Vincent.

3

When she awoke Marion found that Rebbie had already got up, and she slipped leisurely out of bed and began to dress. A glance from the window showed her that the weather hadn't improved, but at least it wasn't foggy, so perhaps they would have an easy night. She smiled at the optimistic thought. It was always the first conscious thought in her mind when she awoke, but this time it was hurriedly pushed aside by more important issues. A picture of Alan Vincent slipped into her mind, and she paused and stared dreamily from the window. Was it really true that Alan had asked her out, or had she just dreamed it? For a few moments she was not really sure, but when she had convinced herself that it had happened the night before she finished dressing hurriedly, and there was an impatience inside her to get on duty in order to see him again.

Rebbie Norris came into the room, smiling widely, and Marion wondered what had pleased her friend, although Rebbie was always smiling.

'So you're up!' Rebbie closed the door and leaned against it, her large figure relaxed after a day's refreshing sleep. 'I thought you would never come to, the way you were sleeping when I left the room. I'm ready to go and eat. I'm famished. What about you?'

'I've got the same complaint,' Marion admitted with a smile.

'And you look pleased with yourself,' her friend noted. 'I don't wonder at it, taking Alan Vincent off the list the girls have got made out. You'd better treat him right or they'll all be after your blood.'

'I suppose I shall get my leg pulled for a bit,' Marion said as they left the room. 'But I don't mind that. I've been hoping for a long time that Alan would get around to asking me out.'

'Don't boost your hopes too high, my girl.' There was unusual seriousness in Rebbie's voice. 'I don't want to see you get hurt. You're not like some of the other girls, always out with a different man, building up a resistance to the hurts that can come.'

'You talk like a disillusioned old maid,' Marion said with a laugh.

'I know what I'm talking about,' came the swift reply. 'I have savoured the delights of romance, I can tell you, and found them wanting in most cases. There's always a snag or two, or at least that's what I've found. If you get it any different then let me know. But I've found that the majority of men aren't all they suppose themselves to be.'

'Then you haven't found true love yet,' Marion told her wisely. 'When the right man comes along you'll be able to blind yourself to his faults.'

'Listen at you! I think you've been reading too many romantic novels.'

They left the home and went across to the hospital, and as the time for them to go on duty drew near Marion began to feel anticipation wind its tenuous threads through her breast. It was with a feeling of great excitement that she walked along the corridor to the Casualty department, and once inside the familiar surroundings she paused to take stock of the situation. There was an average number of people waiting to see the doctor, and several of the cubicle curtains were drawn, an obvious sign that patients were within, waiting to be seen.

Staff-nurse Jannis appeared from one of the cubicles, and the girl appeared harrassed. She smiled at Marion, and took a deep breath as she paused.

'Am I glad to see you!' she said. 'I've been run off my feet. There was a nasty accident between a bus and a lorry in Denton Street about an hour ago. We're just finishing work on the patients who came to us. There were so many injured that some of them were sent to the Infirmary for emergency treatment. Nothing really serious among any of them, but a lot of cuts from broken glass. The driver of the bus and the driver of the lorry are in a serious condition, but most of the passengers got off lightly.' She paused then, and moved closer to Marion. There was a twinkle in her brown eyes as she nudged Marion with a sharp elbow. 'You're a dark horse, aren't you? I've only just heard about you and Dr Vincent.'

'There's nothing in that rumour,' Marion replied mischievously. 'They're all connecting our names at the moment, but next week it may be you in the thick of it.'

'I wouldn't mind if it did happen like that,' Erika Jannis replied wistfully, 'but he doesn't know I exist. I've been working with him solidly for two hours, and as far as he's concerned I'm faceless and without personality.'

'I know exactly what you mean, because I used to get that impression of him myself,' Marion ventured.

'Used to? So there is something in these rumours!'

'He did ask me out, but that was last

night, and today he might have had second thoughts.'

'He'd be a fool if he did.' Staff-nurse Jannis smiled gently as she looked at Marion's lovely face. 'There must be something wrong with all the doctors in this hospital, the way you've been overlooked. But I think our Dr Vincent is a shrewd man. He's taken a long time to make up his mind which nurse he likes best, but having made it up I'm sure he won't waste any more time. Good luck to you, Marion.'

'Thank you, and somehow I think I'm going to need it,' Marion replied.

The staff-nurse went off duty and Marion hurried around to check everything before going to find Alan Vincent. The last of the causalties from the accident had been attended to, and for the moment there was a lull in the bustling activities that had overwhelmed the department. But a steady stream of out-patients was going into the Consulting-room, and Marion went there, nerves tensed and pulses racing.

Alan was bending over a woman seated on the chair beside the desk, and he was talking soothingly to her, his face intent as he examined the abcess on the woman's forearm. Marion watched him for a moment, admiring him, knowing that his patience was inexhaustible, that he displayed as much consideration for this slight case as he did for any of the major ones. He sensed her presence, and glanced up momentarily, a smile of welcome showing briefly on his handsome face. Marion smiled, and went forward to help.

'Good evening, Nurse,' he greeted formally. 'Not such a bad night out there, is it?'

'Better than last night,' she replied automatically.

'I want Mrs Barnes to have a kaolin poultice on this abcess,' he said. 'Will you take her along to the cubicle? Come and see me again in the morning, Mrs Barnes, and I think matters will have reached a head sufficiently for us to do something about it.'

'Thank you, Doctor,' the woman replied, getting to her feet. 'You're very kind.'

Marion took the woman along to a cubicle and made her comfortable, and fetched one of the Juniors to apply the poultice. She went back to the Consulting-room to escort in the next patient, and found a big man seated in the chair nearest the door. His fleshy face was pale, and there was a big piece of white rag wrapped around his left hand, with bloodstains showing upon it.

'What have you been doing?' Marion demanded, as the man got to his feet.

'I'm a butcher,' he said. 'This isn't the first time I've cut myself, but it's the worst. My fault! I was in a hurry to get some of tomorrow's orders ready, and my hands were frozen from working in the cold store. I didn't feel it at first, and got the shock of my life when I saw the blood spurting.'

'Just wait here a moment and I'll fetch the doctor. I expect we'll have to go into the theatre with you.'

Marion opened the door of the office and Alan Vincent looked up.

'Many more out there?' he demanded.

'About a dozen, but not all of them patients,' she replied. 'The next case is a serious cut.' She gave him the details, and he nodded.

'Take him into the theatre, Marion,' he said, and her heart seemed to skip a beat at the sound of her name on his lips. 'Is he all right? Showing any signs of shock?'

'He's a butcher, and I gather it isn't the first time he's cut himself. He seems quite cheerful.'

'Well keep a close eye on him, just in case. I'll be along there in a moment.'

Marion obeyed, smiling at him as she went out, and her heart seemed to be working overtime as she led the unfortunate butcher into the little operating theatre. When Alan came along he winced at the sight of the gash on the man's hand and forearm, and quickly set to work, and Marion had already prepared the things he might need.

Later, when the last of the out-patients had been attended, there seemed to be a lull, and there wouldn't be much to do for any of them, unless accident cases started coming in. Marion checked that the Juniors were doing their routine work, and went along to the staff office to set about the paper-work that had accumulated. There was a tap at the door just after she had settled down, and she glanced up to see Alan in the doorway.

'Hello,' he commented. 'That's what I'm trying to catch up on at the moment. How are you?'

'Very well,' she replied, smiling, as he came into the office and sat down on a corner of the desk.

'I telephoned my Uncle Jim today,' he announced with a smile. 'He's coming this weekend, and he sounded delighted when I suggested it to him. I'm looking forward to it myself, and I've been racking my brains to think of somewhere suitable that we could go to for the day. Have you got any ideas?

What does your mother like doing?'

'She's like me — very easy to please,' Marion said. 'What about your uncle?'

'He's keen on these old houses and such places. Have you ever visited one?'

'I haven't, but it is the sort of thing that would appeal to me. It wouldn't matter much about the weather, either, would it?'

'Not at all.' He seemed pleased. 'There is a big house just through Colchester. Perhaps we can take it in this weekend. Anyway, we'll see what the others think of it when they arrive. They may have different ideas of what to do.'

'It sounds fine to me,' Marion said contentedly. 'I wish today was Saturday.'

'And so do I.' He glanced down at her, his face relaxed. There was a brightness in his blue eyes that sent a pang through her, and Marion stifled the sigh that came up into her throat. She wanted to keep her feelings secret, because if she showed him that she was intense then he might be scared off. She wanted to know what was in his mind before permitting her own emotions to show, but she was looking forward to the day when he would know something about her, when he might start considering their first kiss.

The jangle of the telephone made Marion start nervously, and Alan got to his feet as she lifted the receiver. He signalled to her that he was going back to the Consulting-room, and closed the door as she nodded.

'Casualty department,' Marion said. 'Nurse Talbot.'

'This is Ken, Marion. Can I come along there and talk to you this evening?'

'Ken!' Marion could not keep the surprise out of her tones. 'But I'm busy,' she objected instantly. 'Is it important?'

'Not to you. But I think it is. I've been hearing all kinds of tales about you today. Is there any truth in the story that you're going around with Alan Vincent?'

'I am not going around with him,

61

Ken,' she replied guardedly. 'You know as well as I do that each week a different girl is linked with him. I suppose it's my turn this week.'

'I'd hate to think that after all the times I've asked you out you'll turn to someone like Vincent,' he persisted. 'He hasn't got a human feeling in his body, Marion. 'He's not interested in girls.'

'To the same extent that I'm not interested in men,' she felt obliged to say. 'Are you off duty, Ken?'

'I am at the moment.'

'And you've been drinking.'

'So what? I've got nothing else to do with my time. I wish I could come along to Casualty and talk to you.'

'Sorry, but that's out of the question. I'm too busy to stop work now. You'd better try and sober up a little, in case you're called out.'

'I'm all right. I'll see you later.'

The line went dead before Marion could say anything more, and she replaced the receiver and sat for a moment, frozen by fast moving thoughts. Surely she was not going to have any trouble from Ken Harland! He might be feeling low because she hadn't accepted any of his numerous offers out, but that happened all the time to men. They got used to it. But Ken was so different in many ways. He was so very quiet and inoffensive, and she had been amazed to guess that he had been drinking. He was on call, she knew, and realized that a lot of trouble could arise if he failed to report if wanted.

But what could she do about it? He would be in the Doctor's quarters, she knew, and hesitated before getting to her feet and leaving the office. She went slowly to the Consulting-room, and paused again before tapping at the door and entering. Her heart was thudding faster than normal as she gazed at Alan, awaiting his attention before speaking. He was scribbling furiously on a report, and she felt the heavy silence in the little room very keenly.

'Hello, Marion,' he said, glancing up at last, and throwing down his pen when he saw it was she. 'Sit down.

Have you done all your work?'

'Not yet. I'm worried, Alan.' She hesitated over using his name, and saw a faint smile come to his lips.

'What's wrong?' he demanded. 'Anything I can help you with?'

'That telephone call just now.' She was doubtful about explaining things to him, not wanting him to get the wrong idea, but equally, she was afraid that Ken Harland might make a fool of himself, and she didn't want him getting into trouble on her account. It was not her responsibility because she had never encouraged him, but she felt responsible. He was obviously attracted to her, and if he needed help then she ought to do all she could to assist. She began very hesitantly to give Alan the details, and he listened silently, nodding when she lapsed into silence.

'I can understand how he must be feeling,' he said. 'You can't be held responsible, Marion. But I appreciate how you feel about it. I'm not busy now, and if you like I'll slip across to the quarters and find out what's happening. If I should be wanted in a hurry then you'll have to give me a ring. But I shan't be long, in any case.'

'Thank you, Alan,' she said warmly. 'I knew you would understand.'

'It's just one of the problems that a beautiful girl has to contend with,' he retorted, grinning, and he got to his feet and came towards her. Marion stepped aside for him to depart, but he held out his hands and slipped his arms around her, taking her by surprise, bending over her and kissing her soundly. Marion almost choked in astonishment, but before she could move, or even think, he had released her, holding her with one steady hand as she almost lost her balance. 'That's another problem a girl like you must face up to,' he went on grimly, but his eyes were sparkling. 'I'm sorry I grew impatient, but I couldn't wait until next week before attempting that. Ordinarily we would have gone out together this evening if I'd asked you last night and you'd agreed, and I could have kissed you goodnight. You would have expected that, wouldn't you?'

'Yes.' Marion spoke doubtfully.

'Well it's not my fault we're both working nights, and I have jumped the gun a bit, but I think it was worth it.' He was grinning now, and Marion laughed, recovering from the shock of his swift action. 'Am I forgiven?'

'Certainly not,' she retorted primly, her face expressionless again, and she saw his eyes widen. 'That was most unfair of you.'

'I'm sorry,' he said quickly.

'And so I should think.' She maintained her expressionless face. 'You knew you were going to do that when you got up from the desk, and that gave you time to prepare to enjoy it. But you took me by surprise, and it was over before I realized what was happening.'

'Is that so?' He stared at her for a moment, then his smile returned. 'Well, I can soon remedy that.' He took her into his arms again, moving slowly, intent upon giving satisfaction, and Marion closed her eyes as he kissed her. Fire seemed to flame through her, and she felt burning sensations in her breast. She had dreamed of this so many times, and it had always been a remote desire, but now it was actually happening to her, and the sensations were more powerful than she had ever imagined they could be.

For a timeless period they remained locked in embrace, and Marion felt that her senses were slipping away, taking with them the harsh reality of their surroundings. Then she heard a discreet cough, and struggled to break out of the circle of Alan's arms. Her brown eyes widened in horror when she glanced towards the door and saw that it was open, with one of the Juniors standing there, staring with wide eyes and some embarrassment upon her pretty face.

'Don't you ever knock on doors, and wait?' Alan demanded.

'I'm sorry, Doctor, and Nurse,' came the swift reply, 'but it was urgent, and I didn't stop to think. The emergency alarm is out of order, and the ambulance has been called out. Would you please hurry?'

'Certainly. Come along, Marion! Nurse, ring the Night Sister and tell her we're going out on a call. She'll have someone cover this place.'

Marion almost ran from the room, noting, despite her hurry, the glint in the eyes of the Junior, who was the one she had spoken to about being kissed by the porter in the theatre the previous evening, and she knew her reputation would be torn to shreds in the morning when word of it got out, but she did not care. Grabbing her cape, she hurried out to the ambulance, and there was a singing in her heart and a lightness in her breast that seemed to carry her romantic self high above the plane of routine. Two kisses from Alan Vincent in one evening! The thought was high in her mind. And there would have been more but for the interruption!

The ambulance sped along through

the darkness, and Marion watched Alan's grim face as he checked through the treatment bags. His professional self was to the fore now, and when he glanced at her she could see none of the bright emotion which had been in his blue eyes when he had kissed her.

'We're going to the railway station,' he said curtly. 'A woman has fallen in front of a train.'

'Oh.' Marion could not prevent a shudder. That sort of thing was always so messy. It was not so bad if the person fell between the lines. She pulled her imagination up short, and stifled the feelings that rose inside her. She was a nurse, and if she concentrated upon her work, she would not have time to think of the situation.

The driver was sending the ambulance along as fast as he dared, and the shrill, insistent ringing of the bell seemed to stretch Marion's nerves. Once the ambulance lurched, and there was the squeal of brakes as the driver took avoiding action when another vehicle got in his way. Then they were pulling into the station, and a constable was waiting to direct them to the scene of the action.

Alan carried a bag, and Marion followed behind quickly, catching the constable's words as he gave Alan a picture of the sitaution.

'It's bad,' she heard. 'One of her legs is off. My mate has applied a tourniquet, but he can't stop the bleeding. Have you got some blood?'

'We'll have to check her group first,' Alan replied crisply. 'Are there any other injuries?'

'Her head has taken a hard knock. My mate thinks her skull is fractured.'

Marion glanced back and saw the ambulance driver and his mate coming along with a stretcher. They crossed a platform, and a small group of people were standing behind a temporary barrier, kept back by a police constable. A diesel train stood at the platform, and there were several men on the edge of the platform just in front of the train.

'They were just stopping at the

platform when she fell,' their guide said. 'The train stopped within feet, and backed off after someone checked that she wasn't still across the line. We've done what we could.'

The men moved back a little when they saw the doctor and Marion's uniform. Alan handed his bag to the policeman and jumped down on to the line. Someone had brought up an arc lamp that the railwayman used at scenes of breakdowns or rail crashes, and garish light flooded the figure of the woman lying between the tracks. There were two policemen bending over her, and someone had fetched a car rug to cover her. Alan turned quickly to help Marion down to the track, then took his bag and hurried to the woman's side. Marion followed him quickly, and she was appalled to see the woman's amputated leg lying outside the track. It had been cut off cleanly above the knee, as if a surgeon had operated, and she saw with a twist of emotion that the stocking and shoe were still upon it.

Alan was already making a swift examination. The two constables moved back slightly, and one of them nodded at Marion. They were both soaked in the woman's blood, and their faces were pale and tense in the bright light that glared down at them from the platform.

'I've managed to stop the bleeding,' one of them said, and pulled back the rug that covered the unconscious woman.

'Good,' Alan said, glancing at the leg. 'You've done a good job.' He was more concerned at the moment with what other injuries the woman might be suffering.

Marion moved in beside him, ready to do whatever he asked. The ambulance men came up with the stretcher, and Alan signalled for them to join him on the track. There was a hypodermic in Alan's hand, and he gave the woman a shot of morphine. When he had satisfied himself that she could be moved he checked the leg, and decided that the tourniquet would hold until they got the woman to hospital.

With many hands willing to help, the victim was lifted gently to the stretcher and raised to the platform, and the ambulance men hurried to the ambulance. A moment later they were travelling back the way they had come, and Alan worked swiftly, doing what he could, and it seemed that they had arrived in time . . .

4

Back at the hospital the woman was carried into the little theatre, and help was summoned as the preliminaries were begun. The victim was deeply shocked, and apart from the amputated leg there were signs of a skull fracture. An emergency operation would have to be performed after the leg had been treated. Sister West, in charge of Casualty, came after an urgent telephone call, and she quickly assumed command. Alan scrubbed and dressed for the operation, and he called Marion to him as he prepared to operate. Hubert Waldron, the anaesthetist, came in through the doorway and immediately to the anaesthetic machine. Sister West was on the telephone, arranging for a blood sample to be taken from the woman and supplies of blood to be brought in.

Marion,' Alan said quietly. 'Ken Harland is supposed to be here. He's standing by tonight. We were talking about him earlier, remember? You'd better go and look him up. Tell him to get here at once. I shall need help.'

'But if he's in no condition, Alan?'

'Drunk, do you mean?' His blue eyes were expressionless. 'That's more than likely, but the damned fool should know better than to drink while he's on duty. Go and find out, will you? If he is the worse for drink then leave him where he is, and I'll try to work without him. But if someone misses him, or discovers the state he's in, then he'll be for the high jump, and we'll be able to do nothing to help him.'

Marion nodded and hurriedly left the theatre. She almost bumped into Sister West, her superior, who reached out and grabbed her.

'There's no need to run, Nurse,' came the harsh order. 'I expect everything is under control now. Where are you going?'

'To find Dr Harland, Sister.'

'Go back into the theatre and take your place. You're the senior nurse on duty. The Juniors can't be expected to handle your work. You should have sent one of them for Dr Harland. But I'll ring Switchboard for him. They'll be able to find him. He may be busy in one of the Wards.'

'Yes, Sister.' Marion knew better than to argue with Sybil West. The Sister was hard as nails, and a strict disciplinarian. She was the terror of the Juniors, and made the lives of the Seniors most unpleasant at times with her sergeant-major tactics. Marion hurried back into the theatre, going to scrub up and gown herself. When she approached the operating table Alan was already busy on the patient, and there was tense silence in the brightness of the overhead lamps.

'How is she?' Alan's voice was curt as he spoke to the anaesthetist without looking up. As Casualty Officer Alan was a competent surgeon, and he had handled some remarkable cases in the big theatre in the hospital. But Marion could see that he was worried. Shock had taken a great hold upon the patient, and Marion found herself wondering about the strange woman. Had she fallen in front of the train by accident, or had she tried to commit suicide?

'Pressure is up a bit,' the anaesthetist replied calmly. 'Be as quick as you can, won't you?'

The quietly spoken words gave them all the answer to the question bothering them. Would the patient make it? If Hubert Waldron was worried by the time it might take to perform the operation then the chances of survival were slim. Marion glanced towards the transfusion equipment. The patient's blood had been matched and a bottle was already dripping life-preserving blood into the patient's veins to balance the amount that was being lost. Another bottle was ready to be switched into the circuit of tubing.

The minutes seemed to flit by, yet time was non-existent for them. The silence was heavy, and tension filled them. Drama was present in the brightly lit room, and the assembled skilled people working to save the stranger's life were feeling the effect of it, but nothing showed in their actions, and for all the expression in Alan's pale eyes he might have been at his desk writing a dreary report rather than operating to save a human's precious life. But Marion knew what he was feeling, and admiration filled her as she paused to watch his skilled, unhurried movements.

Sister West came into the theatre, and she moved to the anteroom to scrub and gown herself. Marion watched the older woman thoughtfully, and wondered if Ken Harland was on his way down. She suppressed a sigh as the Sister came back to the table, her mask covering her face, but her blue eyes showing baleful intensity.

'All right, Nurse,' she said to Marion,

who moved away to let Sister take her place. 'Dr Harland is busy in one of the Wards,' she reported to Alan, who nodded slightly, not pausing in his delicate work of closing the blood vessels in the amputation. He would have to cut the flesh back from the stump in order to amputate another short length of the femur, and then he would fold back the flesh to pad the end of the bone. The skull fracture would have to wait until the patient had recovered from the shock of the accident.

Marion glanced at the clock on the wall. It was just past midnight. She felt tiredness pulling at her from inside, but her tension was such that she could ignore it. She felt slightly shocked herself, although she was accustomed to all sorts of dreadful sights in the course of her work. She tried to keep her personal self shut out from the front of her mind. That was one of the early lessons to be learned in nursing. One had to go on about the job without letting imagination or emotion take control.

Twenty minutes later Ken Harland walked into the theatre. He paused just across the threshold, and everyone glanced up at him. Marion saw that his face was pale, his eyes ringed with dark circles. He stood straight and steady, looking as if he had been over working, but Marion alone could see that his condition was the result of drinking. She hoped no one else would notice it.

'Do you need my assistance, old chap?' he called to Alan.

'Not if you're busy elsewhere,' Alan replied, pausing for the briefest moment to glance up and gauge Harland's condition. 'I've got over the worst of it. If you've got someone to attend to up in the Wards then go on back to it. I'll let you know if I come across any snags.'

'Very well. I have been rather busy. Let me know if I am needed.' Harland glanced around at the masked faces turned towards him, and he saw Marion. His face seemed to tighten as he turned away, and when the swing door shut behind him the silence rushed back and the operation went on.

'I'm afraid she wont be able to take much more of this,' the anaesthetist called suddenly, and Marion's eyes went automatically to the clock on the wall. Almost one a.m. She took a deep breath as she waited for Alan's reply. The bottle of blood providing the drip in the transfusion was almost empty, and she moved to the machine to be ready to clip in a fresh bottle.

'I'm almost finished here,' Alan said. 'About another ten minutes.'

'It won't be too soon,' Hubert Waldron replied tiredly.

Tension seemed to increase as the remaining minutes ticked away. Then Alan stepped away from the table with a sigh. He glanced around at the attentive faces ringing him, and spoke wearily, feeling the drain of tiredness as his tense muscles relaxed from the ordeal of maintaining strict alertness.

'That's all we can do for her tonight,'

he said. 'There is a skull fracture, but we'll have to wait for X-rays. Sister, get her up to Surgical. There are some empty beds, I believe. I'll have Mr Pacey look at her in the morning.'

A trolley was brought in and the patient transferred to it. When Sister West went out, accompanying the porter, Marion felt a great load lift from her mind. She watched Alan leave, now intent upon writing up his report, and the Juniors began the task of cleaning up. Hubert Waldron was packing away his equipment, and he smiled at Marion. He was tall and thin, with fine features and blue eyes. His crinkly hair was greying at the temples, and at forty-seven he was still a handsome man.

'It's all right for you, Nurse, you're on night duty. But I was on my way to bed when the call came through.'

'Will she live?' Marion demanded.

'Fifty-fifty chance,' he replied. 'She's in a bad way.'

'I wonder if they've found out who she is,' Marion persisted.

'Forget about her,' Waldron said emphatically. 'Prepare for the next casualty. You've been a nurse long enough to know that, haven't you?'

'Yes.' Marion nodded. 'But I can't help thinking sometimes.'

With the theatre restored to its former cleanliness, Marion found time to relax. She went along to the staff office and sat down at the desk. Sister West had gone back to her quarters, and would only be called out again in an emergency, and for the time being Marion was in full charge of the department. She found that she had a headache, and her nerves were overstrung. When she thought of Ken Harland she felt a trickle of anger inside her. He should have been at Alan's side from the moment the patient arrived in the theatre. The operation would have been concluded sooner if he hadn't been drinking, moping over his personal feelings.

There was a tap at the door, and Marion sat up straight and turned around, to find Alan coming into the room. He looked tired, and she uttered an exclamation of horror.

'I've forgotten coffee!' she said. 'What am I thinking of?'

'Don't worry about it,' he replied with a faint smile. 'It has been a nasty experience. I've just asked one of the Juniors to make some coffee for all of us. You're looking pretty ghastly, Marion. Has this case upset you?'

'I don't usually get upset,' she replied gently, 'but now and again we get a case that bothers me. I was concerned about Ken Harland, though. I could tell he had been drinking. It was a good job he didn't get close to anyone. Did you really need him in there, Alan?'

'Not really!' He smiled. 'I'm going up now to have a word with him, though. He'd better watch his step. I can understand his feelings, if he is in love with you but he'll just have to face up to facts. You don't have any feelings for him, do you?'

'I don't, and I've told him that often enough.'

'He's got a responsible position, and he'll have to live up to it,' Alan went on. 'I'm not going to report it this time, but if it happens again there will be trouble. We can't permit anything to endanger the life of a patient. It was really desparate in the theatre for quite some time, and Harland was not in the Wards with another patient. I expect he was trying to sleep it off. I shan't be long. I'm just going across to his quarters to read him the riot act.'

'Be careful!' The words were wrung from Marion's heart.

'What do you mean?' He paused in the act of turning to leave.

'Ken is overwrought at the moment. Wouldn't it be better to leave it until the morning?'

'You could be right!' He nodded slowly. 'I'll go chase up the coffee. You sit here and take it easy. I'll bring you a cup. You've got nothing to do for the moment, have you?'

'Not right now,' Marion said slowly, and he smiled gently as he opened the door. He went out, and as he closed the door at his back Marion heard a loud voice out in the corridor. She frowned and got quickly to her feet, going out behind Alan, and she found him in the passage, facing an unsteady Ken Harland, who was talking loudly in overbearing tones. A coldness swept through Marion as she picked up the truculence in Harland's voice, and she could tell by the stiffness in Alan's shoulders that he was angry.

'So that's where you spend your time when you're not busy,' Harland was saying. 'Holding hands in the office.'

'You'd better shut up and go back to your quarters, Harland,' Alan replied firmly. 'The least said about anything that's happened this evening the better.'

'What the devil do you mean by that?'

'You know very well. Now run along. There's nothing for you here. If I should need you then I'll ring for you.'

'I want to talk to Marion,' Harland said. 'You think you can stop me?'

Marion saw one of the Juniors peering at them from the treatment room, and she compressed her lips as she went forward.

'Ken, why don't you do as you're told?' Her voice held a faint tremor. 'Alan has saved you from a lot of trouble as it is. Don't try to make any more.'

'What trouble?' Harland demanded. 'I'd like to know what you're talking about.'

'Then I'll tell you.' Alan's voice was firm. 'When you came into the theatre to assist me you were in no condition to do so. You've been drinking, and you've taken too much. Its plain to see now that you've had too much. I suggest you go back to your bed and sleep it off, and I'll make arrangements to cover your duties. If anyone wants to know why then tell them you felt ill.'

'I don't want any favours from you, Vincent.' Ken Harland spoke harshly.

'Don't go too far!' Marion warned. 'There are witnesses here.' She glanced towards the treatment room where both Juniors were visible, peering out at the scene.

'I'll see you to your quarters,' Alan said, going forward and putting a friendly hand upon Harland's shoulder. 'Come along. Tomorrow you can talk all you want.'

Marion turned away to go to the Juniors when she saw that Harland was willing to leave, and her heart was pounding heavily as she saw the excitement in the eyes of the nurses. They would have a lot to tell when they went off duty in the morning, she thought coldly. One of them had seen Alan kissing her in the Consulting-room, and now this. Harland's jealousy seemed to know no bounds, and Marion wondered just how much he did care about her.

When there was a scuffling sound, and then a heavy thud, she turned quickly to see Alan sprawled on his back on the tiled floor and Ken Harland standing over him. Horror spurted through her and she turned quickly and ran towards them as Alan pushed himself to his feet. Harland swung a blow at Alan, who avoided it and pinned his man against the wall. Harland began shouting, and Marion winced when she saw him begin struggling with Alan, who stepped away quickly and planted his feet firmly on the floor in order to swing a shrewd blow to Harland's stomach. Harland collapsed suddenly, like a sack of potatoes falling, and as silence returned to the corridor Marion became aware that someone was standing near the door of the theatre, watching the whole thing. She compressed her lips when she recognized the porter, Martin Salmon.

Alan bent over Harland and began raising him to his feet. Marion went forward quickly and tried to help, but Harland was heavy, and although he was not unconscious he could not help himself as yet. The porter came along quickly, an expression of enquiry on his face, and he moved in and took hold of Harland, helping Alan to half carry his burden into the treatment room.

'Call in the Juniors,' Alan said to Marion. 'We'd better try and sort this out before anything further happens.' He bent to examine Harland, who was groaning softly.

Marion went to the door and summoned the two nurses, who were standing in the corridor, watching and waiting with wide-eyed interest. They followed Marion without comment, and Alan looked up at them.

'I presume that you all saw what happened out there,' he said gently. 'I think the best thing we can do is forget that it happened. Mr Harland hasn't been himself all evening, and I'm sure you understand. If a report were made then someone might lose his job, and there could be embarrassment for the rest of us.'

'I didn't see anything, Doctor,' the porter said, glancing at the Junior nurse with whom he had been in the theatre. 'I know that Nurse Talbot turns a blind eye at times, so the rest of us can do the same.'

'Good. Now when he recovers his senses a little more perhaps you would see him back to his quarters.' Alan spoke softly. 'I don't want to upset him any more, but I'll have a word with him tomorrow morning. If anyone should see you helping him just say that he's been taken ill, that I've seen him and ordered him to bed, and that I shall be covering his duties for the rest of the night.'

'Leave it to me, Doctor,' the porter said with the ghost of a smile playing around his lips.

Harland was now taking notice of what was going on around him. He tried to get to his feet, and Alan stepped back out of the way as the porter put a helping hand to his colleague's shoulder. But Harland shrugged him away, and looked first at Marion, then at Alan.

'I'm sorry for what happened,' he said.

'Nothing happened,' Alan told him politely. 'You're not feeling well. Go back to bed. I'll stand in for you until morning.'

'Thanks, I'll do that.' Ken Harland

turned away and staggered through the doorway. He didn't look back, and Alan motioned for the porter to follow him.

Marion sighed her relief as the two nurses followed the porter, and she watched Alan's face. His bottom lip was beginning to swell, she noticed, and his face was pale. He turned to her, smiling briefly.

'Well things do happen around this department at night,' he commented. 'How does it feel to have two men fighting over you?'

'It was dreadful,' she replied quickly. 'I only hope we can hush it up. There would be a lot of trouble for everyone if it got out.'

'Harland may not even remember it in the morning,' he said. 'I think our own staff will be loyal to us, but we can't afford to have secrets flying around here. We could leave ourselves open to blackmail if we're not careful.'

'The nurses aren't like that,' Marion said hopefully. 'I think they'll forget the incident.'

'Let's hope Harland will!' Alan rubbed his jaw reflectively. 'He hit me hard. I wasn't expecting it, but I should have been on guard. He must think an awful lot of you, Marion.'

'It isn't my fault,' she retorted. 'I haven't given him any encouragement.

'You don't have to encourage anyone,' he said softly, taking her hand. 'Look what you've done to me. I've been impervious to all females, but you walked right through my defences and stabbed me to the heart. Now where were we when the alarm went?' He stared at her closely, a gleam in his blue eyes, and Marion felt her heart skip a beat.

'You were kissing me in the Consulting-room,' she replied evenly, 'and we were disturbed.'

'Just wait until I get a free evening, and you're off duty,' he promised. 'I shall see to it that we don't get disturbed.'

The distant jangle of an ambulance bell alerted them, and Marion suppressed a sigh as she left the room and went along to see what was coming in. The Juniors were already at the outer door, and there was the sudden glare of lights as the vehicle outside swung around to present its tail to the door. As Marion reached the doorway the ambulance men appeared with a stretcher, and behind them came a policeman holding a large handkerchief to his forehead and one eye. He was minus his helmet, and Marion could see a lot of blood on his chest and shoulders. She hurried forward to take charge of him.

'Take the stretcher into the first cubicle,' Marion ordered and already Alan was coming along the corridor to see what was happening. Marion took the constable's arm and led him towards the treatment room, and one of the Juniors moved in on the other side.

They helped the constable to a seat, and Marion gently prised his fingers away from the bloodied handkerchief he was pressing against his head.

'Let me have a look,' she commanded gently, and he relaxed in the seat with a long sigh escaping him.

'I'm all right,' he muttered as Marion examined the large bruise on his forehead. There was a long deep gash in his scalp, and this was bleeding copiously. 'It's my mate I'm worried about. He's been shot.'

'Don't talk now,' Marion soothed. 'We'll soon have you patched up, and your colleague is in good hands.' She motioned to the Juniors. 'Clean him up, will you, and the doctor will see him shortly.'

She left the room and went along to the cubicle. The two ambulance men were standing outside, and they were grave-faced. Marion nodded to them and lifted aside the curtain, entering the cubicle to find Alan bent over the figure of the patient.

'Gunshot wound,' he commented, glancing up at her. 'But it doesn't seem to be very serious. The bullet is very small, and it's lodged just under the shoulder. I don't think it's too low! I hope not, anyway. Will you prepare the theatre for immediate surgery. We'll have to remove the bullet.'

'Right away,' Marion said. She paused as she departed. 'Will you want Sister West here?'

'No, we can handle this ourselves.' He smiled at her, but glanced down quickly when the patient moaned. 'He's coming to,' he commented. 'How is the other one?'

'He sustained a heavy blow to the forehead,' Marion reported. 'He's lost a lot of blood, but he doesn't seem to be too badly hurt. You'll have to do some needlework on him though.'

'I was hoping this would turn out to be a quiet night,' he said, shaking his head. 'But someone has been getting even more excitement than we've had here.'

Marion went on her way, checking with the nurses in the treatment room before going on to the theatre. She took the instruments up and prepared a tray, and Alan appeared as she satisfied herself that everything was in readiness.

The patient was wheeled in, and one of the Juniors entered.

Removing the bullet proved uncomplicated, and Alan was satisfied as he bandaged the wound. The patient was groaning as he was wheeled from the theatre, and Marion went to the treatment room to fetch the other constable. There was a uniformed sergeant there, talking to his injured subordinate, and the sergeant followed them as they went into the theatre. He never stopped asking questions while Alan stitched the head wound, and Marion learned that the plain-clothes constable had been investigating a car theft when his suspect drew the gun and shot him. The uniformed man had come round the corner into the street at that moment, and had been felled with a blow from the pistol. A full scale search was going on for their attacker.

Marion glanced at the clock on the wall and saw the time was just two-thirty a.m.!

5

With both patients treated and the police gone about their business, the department seemed to settle down again, and Marion was relieved that the rest of the night was uneventful. She was not sorry that it was time to go off duty, and such was her mental exhaustion she felt disinclined to go along to the dining room for a meal, unwilling to face the barrage of questions which would surely come from the night-staff. But she met Rebbie Norris in the corridor outside the department, and her friend took her arm and refused to listen to objections as she walked towards the dining room.

But the two juniors mentioned nothing about the trouble that had occurred in the department between Alan and Ken Harland, and Marion was genuinely relieved that wisdom had sealed their lips. There was a lot of shop-talk, and the Juniors lost no time in talking about the patients they'd had during the night.

After the meal Marion walked with Rebbie across to the home. She was silent, feeling slightly depressed by the events of the night, but she could not remain dispirited very long. All she had to do was recall the way Alan had kissed her. That brought the gleam back to her eyes, and she found herself joking with Rebbie as they prepared to go to sleep . . .

The rest of the week seemed quiet after the hectic cases that had passed through the department earlier. Marion found each day passing in succession, and the nights were no longer a tiresome duty but a wonderful chance to see Alan and begin to learn about him. Thursday night seemed the longest, but when she went off duty on Friday morning, Marion knew that the near future would bring untold happiness. There was a deal of promise in Alan's eyes as he spoke to her shortly before the day-staff came on duty.

'I shan't be seeing you this evening,' he said. 'But I have arranged to be on hand to meet Uncle Jim. He'll be arriving at the Regent Hotel some time tonight. I don't know exactly when. I hope you'll find your mother well, Marion.'

'Thank you, Alan. I'm sure she's very excited now. Perhaps I can talk her into moving nearer to me. There are several flats for rent in the neighbourhood, and if she moved here I'd go and live with her instead of staying at the home.' She laughed lightly. 'I hope you'll like her, Alan.'

'I hope she'll like me!' he retorted with a grin, and Marion went off duty with an unusual lightness, a great sense of anticipation in her breast.

She slept through the day as usual, and awoke during the afternoon to find Rebbie getting dressed. Pushing herself up on one elbow, Marion glanced at her watch. Three-thirty! There was enough time for her to dress leisurely and have tea. Her mother wouldn't be arriving until six. She would go down to the railway station to meet her.

'Your mother comes today,' Rebbie commented. 'Are you goint to introduce Alan to her?'

'His uncle is coming here for the weekend as well,' Marion explained. 'I expect we'll all get together.'

'That will be nice, but if I were in your shoes I'd want to be alone with Alan Vincent.'

'Plenty of time for that,' Marion replied with a smile. 'I don't want to rush him. I have a sneaking suspicion that he's a little bit shy, so I'll have to handle him gently.'

'That's right. Never rush the first obstacles.' Rebbie was grinning. 'I can see that you don't have anything to learn, my girl. But what about Ken Harland?

'What about him?' Marion sat very still. Nothing had been said about the incident which had occurred in Casualty, and afterwards, seeing Ken around the hospital, Marion had passed the time of day with him and he had replied as if nothing had ever happened. But she had been afraid that someone would start talking about it, and each passing day, with no gossip reaching her ears, had found her just that little bit more relieved.

'Does he still ask you out?' Rebbie demanded.

'No, not since word got out that Alan has asked me out.'

'Some men are easily discouraged,' the girl remarked with a smile and a shake of her fair head.

Marion dressed slowly and prepared to go out. She disliked waking up after a night of duty. Time seemed upside-down, and when the next meal came it was tea instead of breakfast, and that always seemed unnatural to her. But this time it didn't matter. She whiled away the time until she was almost too late, and then she hurried to the station to meet her mother.

At the station she found that the train would be late, and paced the platform, recalling the incident of the woman falling beneath the train. She suppressed a shudder at the grim pictures that came floating into her mind, and was glad that the woman was beginning to show some slight improvement in her critical condition. Marion always made a point of asking about patients who came into her hands, and it was always a relief to her when she learned that the emergency work that she did helped to save precious lives.

The train came in at last, and Marion stood at the barrier anxiously studying the faces of the passengers as they came along the platform. Then she saw her mother, and waved eagerly, her face showing happiness but her eyes narrowed critically. She didn't like the pinched look about her mother's face, but there seemed nothing wrong as they greeted each other. Marion threw her arms around her mother's neck, and they kissed fondly before standing back to look at one another.

'You're not looking too well now,

Mother,' Marion said severely. 'Are you sure you're taking good care of yourself?

'I am, dear,' Mrs Talbot replied. She was tall and good-looking and it was easy to see that they were mother and daughter. They both had the same dark eyes and good features, but there were streaks of grey showing now in Mrs Talbot's well kept hair. 'Have you any news to tell me? Anything out of the ordinary? I've had a strange feeling all this week, and today couldn't come quick enough for me.'

'I know just how you feel,' Marion said, taking her mother's suitcase. 'Come along and we'll go to the hotel and get you settled in. There's quite a lot I do want to tell you and I promise that you'll be pleasantly surprised.'

'You've found someone!' Mrs Talbot said eagerly, as they left the station, and Marion smiled as she signalled for a cab.

'I didn't know anyone had been lost,' she commented.

'You know what I mean, Marion,' her mother said firmly. 'I am getting worried about you! At twenty-three you should start taking an interest in men. I know you've been very busy for the last five years or so. It isn't easy studying to be a nurse, but all that is behind you now, and you must be getting some time to yourself.'

The taxi took them to the hotel, and Mrs Talbot liked the room they were shown into. Marion helped her mother to settle in, and then they sat down and talked. Mrs Talbot wanted to know everything, but Marion kept putting off the moment of talking about Alan. Then before she could broach the subject there was a tap at the door, and she started almost sheepishly to her feet, recalling that Alan had promised looking in on them as soon as he had met his uncle.

'I'll go, Mother,' she said quickly. 'I think I know who it might be.'

'You've arranged for someone to call?' There was a twinkle in Mrs

Talbot's dark eyes. 'I can tell by your face that something momentous is taking place in your life right now, and it can only be a man! Don't keep me in suspense, Marion. Open the door.'

'If it is Alan, then treat him gently,' Marion pleaded. 'He is so very sensitive.'

Mrs Talbot smiled as Marion crossed the room and opened the door. Her intuition had been a good guide, and she was relieved and happy for her daughter. Marion opened the door with her heart beating fast, and she smiled when she saw Alan standing there, a tall, broadshouldered good-looking man behind him.

'Hello, Marion,' Alan said easily. 'So your mother has arrived safely.' He half turned towards the man with him, whose blue eyes were already critically studying her. 'Uncle Jim — Marion Talbot. I hope you'll take to each other because we're all going to spend Sunday together.'

Marion smiled as she held out her

hand, and it was shaken in a firm grip.

'Pleased to meet you, Marion,' Jim Vincent said. 'I just had to come along this weekend to meet you after all Alan has told me about you. I thought he must be exaggerating, but I'm glad to report that he has told the truth. You are everything he says.'

'Thank you,' Marion replied, smiling. 'Please come in. My mother doesn't know about you yet, Alan, and she's in for quite a surprise.'

He smiled as she stepped back and opened the door wide, and he led his uncle into the room. Mrs Talbot was standing by the small table, a smile of welcome upon her attractive face, and her eyes showed the degree of happiness which she was feeling at this moment. Marion introduced Alan, who in turn introduced his uncle, and in a very short while they were all talking easily. Marion was surprised and pleased to find that Alan was not awed by her mother, as she had half-expected that he might be, for she had been convinced for a long time that Alan was shy, or at the very best, reserved. However he displayed no symptoms now, and kept the conversation going quite well. But he had little time to spare, and soon made his apologies.

'If I'm to be left on my own now I'm here, and you two ladies have made no arrangements for the evening, then let me play host to you,' Jim Vincent said. 'If we are to be companions this weekend then let's well and truly break the ice before the great day arrives.'

'I shall be delighted,' Mrs Talbot said quickly, before Marion could make any reply. 'We'll take good care your uncle, Alan.'

'I wish I could take advantage of the same offer,' Alan said with a rueful smile. 'But someone has got to do the work. However you must take it easy, Jim, because Mrs Talbot has been ill.'

'I'm quite all right now,' Jessica Talbot said, and Marion shook her head in wonder as she moved to the door to show Alan out. She was certain that her mother was prepared to flirt with Jim Vincent!

'This will do Uncle Jim some good,' Alan said as Marion stepped outside the door with him. 'He leads a lonely life. Shall we concentrate our efforts this weekend upon giving them both a good time?'

'Yes,' Marion agreed. She tremored as he took her hand. There was gentleness in his face, and she knew that her own features showed emotion. There was a subtle stirring inside her, as of the first movement of Spring, she imagined, and she knew that her heart was letting her become involved deeply with this handsome young man. She had begun to think that it would never happen to her, but it was reality now, and she could only bless her good fortune and hope that it would remain constant.

'I must go now.' He dropped her hand reluctantly. 'Don't make any plans for your free evenings next week, will you?'

'No. I'll keep them all for you.' Marion smiled as he grinned and turned away, and she felt happier than she had ever been. There was no clouds on her horizon, she decided. 'But what about tomorrow?' she called. 'Have you made arrangements for meeting your Uncle?'

'Don't panic.' He chuckled. 'It's all been taken care of. I'll ring him in the morning. I expect you'll be around with your mother. We'll get together, Marion.'

She nodded, and watched him out of sight along the corridor. When she went back into the room and closed the door she found her mother and Jim Vincent chatting together like very old friends.

'Well, what's on the menu for this evening?' Jim Vincent demanded. 'Id like to play host to you charming ladies. I don't see much life where I live, and I jumped at the chance to come here this weekend. You're not feeling too weak for a strenuous evening out, Mrs Talbot?'

'Not at all,' Marion's mother replied, smiling. 'I feel just ready to take up a social life again. I think I've fallen into a rut, and a sharp change now should do me a world of good.'

'Then what do you suggest?' His blue eyes reminded Marion of Alan. This cheerful man was very much like his nephew, and some of their mannerisms were similar. 'I don't think we should go out to paint the town red, but we can have some fun. You should know all the bright spots, Marion.'

'I'm afraid I don't!' Marion shook her head ruefully. 'I haven't found the time or the inclination to whoop it up.'

'Then you don't know what you've been missing.' His eyes were alight with pleasure. 'It's a pity that Alan can't be with us this evening, but I'll make a competent stand-in, never fear. Is it too late to try and see a show? There must be something worth-while going on in this place. Then we could visit the smartest restaurant, or a club, if there is one. We'll do it in style, and I shall have the time of my life escorting two very lovely women.'

Marion watched her mother's face,

seeing the pleasure dawning in her blue eyes, and she nodded. It would do them all good to have a night out.

'I hope it won't be too much of a rush for you to get ready, Mrs Talbot,' Jim Vincent said. 'I'll go along to my room and ring for service and try to find out what's happening in Ambury tonight. Then I'll call a cab and have it pick us up in twenty minutes. Will that be sufficient time for you?'

'I'll be ready in ten,' Jessica Talbot said lightly, and Marion was surprised to note that her mother suddenly seemed ten years younger.

'You already look like a picture, Marion,' Jim Vincent said boldly. 'I admire Alan's taste, I must say.' He moved towards the door. 'In twenty minutes then.'

'We'll be ready and waiting for your knock at the door,' Mrs Talbot promised.

'That will be worth seeing,' he retorted with a smile.

'Mother, are you sure you want to go

gallivanting all over town, after a tiring trip here?' Marion demanded after the door had closed behind Jim Vincent.

'My dear, I wouldn't miss this evening for anything,' her mother replied. 'I feel better already. I think this weekend is going to be a most memorable one. Now unpack my case for me, dear, while I freshen up. We mustn't keep Mr Vincent waiting.'

'What did you think of Alan?' Marion asked diffidently, and saw her mother smile knowingly.

'I think you've picked a winner, dear! I like him. I can judge a person at first sight, as you well know, and I have no fears about Alan Vincent. Is he getting serious?'

'I wouldn't know about that! We haven't even been out together yet. He only asked me during the week, and we've both been on night duty ever since. Next week should see us getting together.'

'Well, I shall keep my fingers crossed for you, Marion. I think you deserve someone like Alan Vincent. Perhaps I should try and take his uncle out of the way on Sunday. That would give the two of you some time together.'

'No, don't do that,' Marion begged. 'Alan and I have decided that we should make this weekend a special one for you and his uncle. It will also help break what little ice there is left between us. I think he's a bit shy. He hasn't taken out a single girl since he's been at the hospital.'

'Does that mean he might have taken out a married one?' Mrs Talbot's eyes were sparkling with good humour, and Marion felt a sudden warmth flood her. She had been worried about her mother's health, but here was proof that Mrs Talbot was completely well.

'You'd better hurry up and get ready,' she said, turning to open her mother's case. 'Better not keep Mr Vincent waiting. I'll have everything put away by the time you are ready.'

'This evening will make me feel quite young again,' Mrs Talbot remarked, disappearing into the bathroom.

It was a wonderful evening, Marion decided long before it was over. Jim Vincent was as good as his word and arranged everything. They went to see a show, and afterwards were taken to a restaurant, where the sky was the limit as far as Jim Vincent was concerned. He was very attentive, and Marion found herself liking him immensely. They had a good meal, and some delightful wine and Marion found herself slipping into unreality. There was a sense of anticipation inside her for the weekend, and she knew instinctively that Alan Vincent was going to become very important to her. Perhaps Jim Vincent sensed it also, for he made great efforts to entertain them, and when at last they began to think of returning to the hotel, Marion felt that she had never enjoyed herself so much.

Seated in the taxi, with Jim Vincent between them, Marion glanced at her mother's gentle face in the gloom, and she knew that her life was changing, that by Monday nothing of the old impressions would be left. The future was going to be gloriously different. Happiness was piling up, and the man she had so often wished would notice her was going to get very serious about her. She knew that as if he had told her, and the memory of his lips against her mouth sent the sensations shuddering through her.

'I've had a most enjoyable evening,' Jim Vincent remarked as they were whisked back to the hotel. 'I've had the best of company, and I shall make Alan envious when I tell him about it. But he'll have his turn tomorrow evening. I understand that he's organizing everything. I hope I haven't been a bore, ladies.'

'Far from it,' Mrs Talbot said quickly. 'I've never enjoyed myself more. I'm going to be very sorry when this weekend is over, Mr Vincent.'

'Call me Jim,' he said happily. 'I know just what you mean. I live a humdrum life, running my small business. That's all life seems to consist of these days, working and sleeping, working and sleeping. I can see that I'll have to visit Alan more often, and I think you should see your daughter at least once every month. Perhaps we can make it the same weekend every time!'

'That sounds a very good idea.' Mrs Talbot leaned forward to look at Marion. 'What do you say, dear?'

'Go ahead and make your arrangements,' Marion told them. 'I'm sure Alan will be pleased with anything you say.'

'We'll go into it later.' There was a trace of regret in Jim Vincent's voice as he looked up and saw the hotel looming up at their side. The cab stopped and the driver got out to open the door for them. Rain was misting down, reinforcing the dampness on the pavements, and Marion shivered slightly as she took her mother's arm and walked her into the hotel vestibule. Jim Vincent joined them almost immediately, smiling broadly, and he sighed audibly. 'So the evening has come to an end,' he remarked. 'That's a pity, but we have plenty of time left, haven't we? I have to telephone Alan at the hospital in the morning, so what shall I tell him? Or shall I see you in the morning before I call him?'

'That will be a better idea,' Mrs Talbot said, holding out her hand to him. 'Thank you so very much for such a wonderful time. I have enjoyed myself immensely, and meeting you has been a great pleasure.'

'It was my pleasure entirely,' he retorted, smiling at Marion. 'And I was charged by my nephew to take very good care of you. I hope you'll put in a favourable report about me, Marion.'

'I certainly shall!' Marion took his hand as he extended it, and he gripped her fingers hard.

'I hope you and Alan will become very good friends,' he said, with a little touch of seriousness now in his voice. 'He's a very nice chap. I say that although he is my nephew. He's quiet and dependable, and you're just right for him, Marion. I shouldn't be saying that, mind you, but I think we're friends.' He smiled broadly. 'Now I'll see you to your room, Mrs Talbot. Are you returning to the nurses' home, Marion'

'Yes. I shall be seeing Mother about ten in the morning.'

'And I hope to see you as well.' He stepped away, making room for Jessica Talbot to precede him to the stairs.

'Goodnight, Mother,' Marion said fondly. 'Sleep well.'

'Have no fears for my beauty sleep tonight,' Mrs Talbot said warmly. 'I'm so tired I can hardly wait for my head to touch the pillow. But I haven't felt as well as this for a very long time. My doctor said this change would do me good, but he had no idea just how true his words were. Goodnight, dear. See you at about ten in the morning.'

Marion stood and watched them out of sight, and there was a happy smile on her lips as she turned slowly to leave.

She went out into the rain and crossed the wide street to the hospital. Her thoughts were deep, running fast through her mind. All the impressions of the evening were gathered inside her, and she knew a deep sense of hope as she pictured Alan's face. If this evening had been wonderful without him how much better would it have been in his company? On Sunday she would be spending the entire day in Alan's company, and at the moment there was nothing she more desired . . .

6

Following the paths around from the hospital, Marion walked in shadows. The lights of the hospital at her back and the glare from the many windows of the home in front of her made a great deception for her eyes, and she was half lost in her thoughts as she followed the route almost instinctively. But the shadows seemed to move to her left as she passed under an archway of trellis. Her heart lurched as a figure appeared from the gloom, and she took a swift breath.

'Marion, I've been waiting to see you.' The voice spoke harshly, but she recognized the tones, and relief swept through her, although she was startled.

'Ken, what the devil are you doing wandering around in the darkness? Are you trying to scare half the nurses in the hospital? You'll be starting rumours about a ghost walking the grounds if you're seen.'

'I saw you go into the hotel a short time ago,' he retorted flatly. 'I must talk to you, Marion.'

'What could be so important?' she asked, and there was a growing coldness inside her. She didn't know what was going on in that mind of his, but he was certainly emotional over her. She thought of the trouble that had blown up the night before in Casualty. That could so easily have gotten out of hand!

'My feelings are important,' he rasped, coming closer. 'I love you, Marion, but you don't seem to care.'

'What can I say to that?' she demanded. 'I don't have any feeling for you, Ken, and that's the truth. It's just one of those things. I am very sorry for you. But you'll just have to try and take your mind off me.'

'I saw you first,' he said thickly. 'Vincent doesn't feel about you the way I do.'

'It isn't a case of first come, first served,' Marion said gently. 'I know you've been asking me out for a long time, but I haven't accepted, and that should prove my feelings. I don't wish to hurt you, but you must pull yourself together, Ken, and try to forget about me. There are other nice girls working at the hospital, and any number of them would be only too pleased to go out with you.'

'It's you I want,' he said quickly, and his strong hands came out of the darkness and grasped her upper arms. He held her tightly, and Marion tried to break his grip without success.

'You're hurting me, Ken,' she said quickly, and there was sharp anger rising inside her. 'Please don't make a fool of yourself. You were in grave danger last night of letting yourself down. Don't do anything for which you may later be sorry. Let me go!'

He pulled her into his arms, and Marion struggled against him. But she was powerless in his hands. His mouth came out of the darkness, finding her cheek, and then her mouth, and she panted as she desperately tried to fight him off. She managed to get a hand free, and slapped his face heavily, but the action only served to anger him, and he grabbed her hard and held her with brute strength.

'You fool!' Marion gasped. 'You'll only make trouble for yourself. Let me go, Ken.'

'I love you, Marion,' he jerked out. His face indistinct in the gloom, but she could see his eyes gleaming in the light coming from the windows of the home, and Marion suddenly had an urgent feeling that he had lost his control. She struggled harder to breakaway from him, but he bent his head over her, kissing her repeatedly, hurting with his passion. They swayed to and fro on the narrow path, and suddenly Marion's foot slipped off the concrete, and her high heel sank into soft earth. They overbalanced and went sprawling over shrubs. Marion landed hard, with

Harland rolling over her, and she sprang up desperately and started running for the home. One of her shoes came off and she realised that she had dropped her handbag, but she kept going, and eventually reached the door of the home, where she paused breathless and filled with panic.

The door opened before she could regain her breath, and a large figure appeared, pausing in the lamplight that shone upon the steps. Marion caught her breath and straightened, pushing back her shoulders. Sister West stared at her, taking in Marion's dishevelled appearance, the fact that she had lost a shoe.

'What on earth has happened to you, Nurse Talbot?' boomed the Sister's loud voice. 'You look as if you've been dragged through a hedge backwards. Have you been involved in an accident?'

'It was nothing,' Marion gasped, steadying herself. She hadn't been afraid of Ken Harland, but she was angry. 'I slipped off the path. You know how dark it is along there. We've been trying to get some lights put up for a long time.'

'Did you hurt yourself?' Sister West reached out and took Marion's elbow in a strong grip. The big woman had almost as much strength as Harland, Marion thought. She was subjected to a close scrutiny under the lamp hanging over the doorway. 'Are you telling me the truth, Nurse?' came the suspicious queston. She broke off when there was a faint sound in the bushes just out of the circle of light. 'Who's there?' she demanded, and Marion half turned to stare into the shadows. 'Have you been attacked by someone, Nurse? Answer me!' Her strong hands shook Marion impatiently.

'There's no one there, Sister,' Marion said quickly. 'I told you what happened.'

'I don't believe you!' Sister West was still staring into Marion's face. 'Either you were attacked or you've been with a man on those paths. Look at your face!

Your lipstick is smeared all over! If you are all right then you'd better caution your boyfriend to have a little more control. Where is your shoe, and did you go out without a handbag?'

'They're still on the path somewhere,' Marion said tiredly. 'I couldn't see them, so I was coming to borrow a torch from Home Sister's office.'

A likely story! When I saw you there was no doubt in my mind that you were running from someone. I've got a good mind to call the police. What on earth has been happening out here? Who have you been with this evening?'

'My mother,' Marion said breathlessly. 'Please leave it alone, Sister. I fell off the path into the wet earth, that's why I'm in such a mess.'

'Wait here and I'll go and get that torch, and I'll have a look around with you,' came the terse reply. Sister West went back into the building, returning a moment later with a long torch, which she switched on and proceeded to use, letting the bright beam flit from bush to bush, probing every shadow. Marion watched tensely, hoping that Ken Harland had the sense to make himself scarce.

They had walked back along the path, and reached the spot where Harland had accosted her. Marion stood watching while the Sister looked around. Her shoe and handbag lay where they had fallen, but the Sister was more interested in the marks on the soft wet soil at the side of the concrete path.

'Here are your footprints,' Sister West announced triumphantly. 'And these beside yours belong to man. You were not alone here, Nurse and I want to know what was going on.'

'Nothing at all,' Marion said slowly. 'There's a turn here in the path, and it's easy to step off the concrete. I expect one of the porters, or a doctor has been along here, and the same thing happened to him that happened to me.'

'I'm not satisfied.' Sister West turned the beam of the torch upon Marion's face. 'What happened here, Nurse? If you have been accosted by someone then don't be afraid to say so. We can't have this sort of thing happening around the hospital.'

'It was nothing like that,' Marion said slowly.

'So you were here with a man. Was it Dr Vincent?'

'Certainly not!' Marion bent to pick up her shoe, which was embedded in the soft soil, and her handbag.

'So it was someone else! You know it isn't permitted to bring men into this part of the hospital. You should have known better, Nurse. I think I'd better report this incident. It should be looked into. I'm not satisfied with your story. Look at your blouse! Its collar is torn! Was someone forcing his attentions on you, Nurse?'

'Sister, nothing like that happened to me!' Marion tried to keep her voice steady. She was wondering if Ken Harland was still around, listening to this conversation, and there was a tingling sensation along her spine as she imagined his passionate eyes staring at her from the shadows.

'You'd better go into the home, and wash yourself clean of that mud,' the Sister said tersely, realizing that she would not get anything more from Marion, but her suspicions were still aroused. 'I'm going to have a good look around, and I'll rouse one of the porters to help me.'

Marion turned and hurried away before Sister West could think of any more questions, and the anger bubbling inside her chased away the panic she had felt. Ken Harland was getting too intense for his own good. He would need a good talking to when he cooled down, and Marion decided to seek him out the next morning. He had to be stopped before he went too far.

Entering the home, Marion hurried to the ablutions, and was in haste to clean herself. She didn't want to show herself in her room in case Rebbie started asking questions. She had put off Sister West, but Rebbie would be a different matter. Her friend would know the signs better than Sister West, and once Rebbie took something into her head she wouldn't let up until she knew all about it.

Feeling cooler after a wash, Marion went along to her room, and was relieved to see that Rebbie Norris was in bed and almost asleep. The girl peered drowsily at her, and smiled, but made no attempt to arouse herself. Marion hurriedly undressed and got into bed, and she lay for a long time in the darkness, awaiting her emotions to subside. Ken Harland hadn't actually frightened her out there on the path, but she had been shaken by the incident, and when she finally drifted into sleep it was with the decision made to speak to him severely next day. The determination was still with her when she awoke the next morning.

Rebbie was about, hurriedly dressing, and Marion glanced at her watch. It was time to get up. She was going to see her mother early, and they would probably go around the town. It would give her an opportunity to do some shopping, and Marion pushed back the bed-covers and arose.

'I've heard some talk about you in the wash room,' Rebbie said severly. 'Having fun and games out on the path last night, weren't you?'

'Are they talking about it already?' Marion gasped.

'Sister West told someone that she saw you coming in looking like you'd wrestled with a bear, and she said she found signs that you had been breaking the rules of the hospital, to wit; a man in your company in the out of bounds area between the hospital and the home. What have you got to say for yourself? Are you guilty, or not guilty?'

'Don't be absurd!' Marion forced a smile that she was far from feeling. She was wondering what Alan would say if he heard such talk! 'I told Sister West that there was nothing in her supposition.'

'You know what she's like! She can't get a man for herself, so she invents all kinds of fantasies. But if she reports you there might be trouble, Marion.'

'Nonsense! What can she report? I appeared before her at the door minus a shoe and my handbag, and I told her that I had slipped off the path in the darkness, that I was coming to get a light so I could look for my shoe and bag. Naturally she didn't believe it. But I don't see what she has to report.'

'She fetched a porter and they searched together, and Sister West swears that she saw a man making off through the shadows!' Rebbie stared hard at Marion's flushed face. 'You can tell me, Marion. Was there anything going on?'

'It was Ken Harland!' Marion compressed her lips as she recalled the incident. 'He was waiting for me to come in, and he took hold of me and kissed me. I tried to push him away and we fell on to the garden. That's all there was to it, but I wasn't going to tell that to Sister West.'

'I should think not. But what on earth is Ken Harland thinking about?' Rebbie Norris shook her head, her blue eyes wide. 'I heard what happened the night before in your department. Fancy fighting among the male staff over you! If that got to Matron's ears there would be some dismissals, I'm sure.'

'That's why I don't want last night's happenings getting out, Rebbie.' Marion spoke severely, and her friend nodded.

'Don't worry about me,' she said with a smile. 'But what are we going to do about Sister West? She's like a terrier. She won't let go until she's satisfied herself that you are telling the truth.'

'I've got nothing else to say on the matter,' Marion said firmly. 'Wait for me to get dressed and we'll go to breakfast.'

She was thoughtful as she prepared to go along to the dining room, and she felt reluctant to face the other nurses, especially with the talk of the blows that were struck between Alan and Ken Harland the previous night going around. On top of what Sister West would have to say about the business of a man in the bushes, Marion realized that there might be some pertinent questions asked of her, and when a staff-nurse came into the dining-room while she was eating her breakfast she guessed that Sister West had made a report about the incident. The staff-nurse came to their table.

'Nurse Talbot, Matron would like to see you in her office at nine-fifteen this morning.'

'Very well, Staff-nurse!' Marion continued with her meal, keeping her eyes upon her plate, trying not to hear the remarks being made by her colleagues at nearby tables.

'Stick to your story,' Rebbie said as they got up to leave. 'They've got no proof. For Heaven's sake don't admit the truth, Marion. Your reputation will be down in the mire if you do.'

'Don't worry about that, Rebbie.' Marion forced a smile. 'Sister West is not going to bully me into anything.'

They went back to their room, and Marion dressed herself for going out.

She was off duty, and wanted to get away as soon as she had faced Matron. But there were butterflies in her stomach as she left the home and walked along the paths to the hospital. She went directly to the matron's office, and didn't have to wait. Sister West was standing outside, and she gave Marion a disapproving stare. Marion sighed to herself, but kept an expressionless face. She had no intention of admitting the incident which had occurred the previous night. That was something which had to be settled between Ken Harland on herself.

Sister West tapped at the door, and entered the office for a few moments, and when she reappeared she beckoned for Marion to go in.

Matron was behind her desk, a tall, slim woman in her early fifties, with bright blue eyes and an engaging smile. But this morning she was serious, and she studied Marion closely for a few moments. Then she spoke.

'Good morning, Nurse Talbot.'

'Good morning, Matron.' Marion was aware of Sister West standing just inside the door at her back.

'I have had a rather serious report of an incident which is supposed to have taken place last night in the grounds of this hospital.' Matron looked at Marion. 'I understand you were connected with this matter, and I should like you to tell me exactly what happened.'

'I'm afraid there's nothing to tell, Matron,' Marion said firmly.

'If the man involved is a member of our staff then you need not worry about shielding him,' Matron said. She placed her hands before her in rather a severe manner, and interlaced her fingers.

'Matron, I'm afraid that Sister West has rather a colourful imagination.' Marion's brown eyes glinted. 'I explained to her at the time just what happened on that path, and she chose to disbelieve me. I have nothing further to say on the matter. I'm sure you've been given a thorough report of what is supposed to have happened, and no doubt you have a note of what I said about it.'

'On the face of it there is nothing more to be said about it,' Matron went on slowly, her voice edged with harshness. 'But there was a witness last night to the struggle you had with some man, and as this witness' report was voluntary, and totally unconnected with Sister West's investigation, it is assumed that there is some substance to Sister West's suspicions. She herself thought she saw the figure of a man leaving the grounds, but could not be sure. However with this other report, I have accepted the fact that there was an assault made upon you. It need not have been anything serious, but the implications are far-reaching. I have the interests of every member of the staff at heart when I say that I want to know exactly what happened.'

The silence that followed Matron's words was heavy and tense. Marion watched Matron's harsh face, and knew that she would have to admit something. There were many nurses at the hospital, and if word went around that some man was molesting the female staff there might be a panic.

'I wasn't attacked or assaulted,' she said slowly. 'It was someone I know well. He wanted to talk to me, and had been waiting for me to come in. I had been out for the evening with my mother.

'I see.' Matron's eyes were narrowed, and they seemed to bore through Marion. 'And this man is a member of the staff?'

'Yes.'

'I would like to have his name.'

'I'm sorry Matron, but I must withhold that. What happened is strictly between the two of us.'

'I'm not certain that I agree with you, Nurse, but if there was no serious attack against you then perhaps it would be as well to consider the matter closed. But I hope incidents of this nature won't occur again. If there is a repetition I shall be required to deal with it most severely. Please bear that in mind, Nurse Talbot.'

'Yes Matron.' There was meekness in Marion's tones, and she kept her eyes lowered. She was thinking of Alan, and wondering what his attitude towards all this might be. If he heard about it there would be more trouble, because he would be sure to speak to Ken Harland about it.

'That will be all, Nurse.' There was no compromise in Matron's stiff tones. It was easy to gauge what she thought about it. Marion left the office with a flush tinting her cheeks, and she was hurrying away towards the exit when Sister West called her back.

'I take a very dim view of this business, Nurse,' the Sister commented heatedly. 'You deliberately lied to me.'

'I did, Sister. It was my own affair, and I knew I could handle it in my own way. There was no need to drag Matron into it. The whole affair was blown up out of all proportion.'

'Well I didn't think so, and I was only doing my duty. I would make the same decision if it happened again. There are a lot of nurses working here, and they have a right to be protected. I don't think your behaviour was far short of being irresponsible. You would be well advised to think carefully next time, before lying to a superior. And you might have the decency to make your male friends behave. Who was the member of the staff with you?'

'Matron has taken this matter as far as she can,' Marion replied firmly. 'There's nothing else to be said.'

'Very well. We'll see about that. You may go.' Sister West turned on her heavy heel and flounced away, and despite her feelings, Marion smiled thinly.

As she was leaving the hospital, a voice hailed her, and she paused and glanced around, her dark eyes shadowing as she saw Ken Harland coming towards her. He was smiling sheepishly, and Marion felt anger rising in her breast. She took a deep breath and tried to count to ten.

'I've been looking everywhere to see you this morning,' he began.

'Listen, Ken,' she retorted firmly, cutting in on him before he could get started with his obviously prepared piece. 'I want to forget what happened last night. There has been too much made of it already, and if we're seen talking the matter might be taken even further. You did a stupid thing last night, and I'll agree to forget it ever happened if you'll come to your senses and promise never to molest me again, in any way.'

'I'm sorry for what happened. I got carried away. But you must understand what I feel for you, Marion. Won't you listen to reason?'

'There's nothing more to be said, Ken. Let's just forget it, shall we?'

'I have plenty to say. I know you're wasting your time with Vincent. I don't want to see you get hurt, Marion. He'll just lead you on. He won't ever get serious about you. I can prove it.'

'Don't be so ridiculous,' Marion replied, trying to hold on to her temper. 'Haven't I made myself clear yet? I don't want anything to do with you. It's as simple as that, and you will have to accept it. If I do have any more trouble from you then I shall go straight to Matron. What happened last night was reported to her, and you can be sure that I shall be watched closely in future. Anyone seen with me, or talking to me as earnestly as you are, will be held suspect. I think they must have a pretty good idea already who was with me on the path last night. Word of what happened in Casualty the other night between you and Alan has got out. We'll all be getting bad reputations if you don't give up.'

'Won't you come out with me just once?' he pleaded 'I could show you such a good time. I'm sure you would change your mind about me after being in my company.'

'I'm sure you're quite a nice person, but there could never be anything between us, Ken. Now I must be going. Please don't make a bigger fool of yourself than you have done already. The other nurses are beginning to talk! You know what that means.'

'Let them!' He was sullen now, his dark eyes bright with controlled emotion. 'I was doing all right with you, Marion, before Vincent started showing an interest. What's he got that I haven't?'

'Good manners for a start,' she replied sharply, and turned away, leaving him standing there with narrowed eyes.

Marion went on out of the main gate and crossed the road to the hotel. She paused in the corridor outside her mother's room for a few moments to try and compose herself, but her heart seemed erratic as she tapped gently at the door.

Mrs Talbot came in answer, and Marion was pleased to see her mother looking so well. She entered the room, and her mother went back to arranging a bouquet of flowers that had just been delivered.

'It's from Jim Vincent,' Mrs Talbot said with a smile. 'We had breakfast together this morning, Marion.'

'No need to apologize, Mother,' Marion

retorted with a smile. 'You're not feeling guilty about it, are you?'

'Good heavens, no! Whatever gave you that idea?' There was the faintest suspicion of a blush appearing on the older woman's face, and Marion went to her mother and put her arms around her.

'Are you enjoying yourself, Mother?' she demanded.

'Very much so, and there's more to come. You should have heard Jim talking at breakfast this morning. He's already spoken to Alan this morning, and between them they've engaged every available moment right up until Sunday night.'

'That sounds hectic.' Marion forced away her feelings. She was feeling depressed by what had happened last evening and this morning, but the thought of seeing Alan, of being with him for many hours over the weekend, was already thrusting feathery sensations through her, and she forgot about Ken Harland and all the unpleasant facts as she began to look forward to the afternoon, when

Alan would be joining them. There was an exciting future stretching ahead of her, and she wanted to exact every ounce of pleasure from it. But she could not help subconsciously worrying about Ken Harland. He had seemed very insistent, and could well do something in his passion which later he might regret!

7

Marion didn't meet Jim Vincent again until after lunch, and when he appeared at the door of her mother's room Alan was with him. Marion quickly searched Alan's face for any sign of worry or tension, wondering if he had heard anything of what had happened the evening before. But Alan smiled easily, and took her hand briefly as he came into the room. Marion was surprised to hear the degree of familiarity in Jim Vincent's voice when he greeted her mother, and she was even further surprised when her ears caught the tone of her mother's reply. Even Alan noticed it because he was quick to make a remark.

'Someone's been wasting no time, Marion,' he said. 'It sounds as if the older generation can teach us a thing or two in making friends.'

'Don't you worry about that,' Jim Vincent said without turning a hair. 'Your mother and I have been getting along famously. I'm sure you two are going to see a whole lot more of us in the future. After this weekend I shan't be satisfied with sitting around at home with nothing but the Sunday papers and television to occupy myself. I'm going to be spoiled by this weekend.'

'A lot of future practices are going to be decided by this weekend,' Alan said lightly, and Marion felt a wave of emotion pass through her breast as she caught his eye.

'Well, what's on the agenda for this afternoon?' she demanded.

'I don't know about this afternoon, but I'm hoping to take your mother out this evening without the two of you tagging along,' Jim Vincent told them, and Marion threw a quick glance at her mother.

'That's right, dears,' Mrs Talbot said sweetly, her face expressionless. 'Jim and I decided that it wouldn't be fair to both of you if we took up all your free time. You and Alan haven't had the time to get out alone together yet, and I'm sure you must both be getting impatient for the opportunity. So Jim and I put our heads together and decided to take control of the whole affair. We shall go out together this evening, leaving you to do the same.'

'Well that's very thoughtful of you, I must say,' Alan said with a grin. 'I was wondering how I could possibly get around to suggesting such an arrangement without upsetting either of you. You're the most understanding mother in the world, Mrs Talbot.'

'Give me some of the credit, Alan,' Jim Vincent said with a smile. 'But let this evening take care of itself. What shall we do this afternoon?'

'I have my car outside,' Alan suggested. 'Shall we go for a drive, and stop at a little country restaurant for tea? I can assure you the food is wonderful, and the atmosphere just perfect.'

'Sounds like a good idea to me,' Mrs Talbot said happily, and no one had any objection.

The afternoon seemed all too slow in passing to Marion, but she tried to concentrate upon the task of entertaining her mother and Jim Vincent, although they seemed happy enough in each other's company. The drive was nice enough, despite the bleakness of the countryside, and when they sat in the little restaurant, which was every bit as fascinating as Alan had promised, rain began to fall.

They had tea, and afterwards sat talking generally. Then Mrs Talbot mentioned Christmas. Which was only just a month away.

'Do you know what duties you'll be doing over the holiday?' she asked.

'Haven't the faintest,' Alan said. 'It's still a bit early for us to get anything finalized. It has only just started filtering into the back of my mind that Christmas is just around the corner. What plans have you made, Jim?'

'None yet,' came the swift reply. 'I

have been thinking about it, and I had been on the point of getting in touch with you to find out what you had in mind. However now the subject has come up we'd better thrash it out.' He turned to Mrs Talbot. 'I suppose you and Marion will spend your time as Alan and I,' he commented. 'We're always very quiet. Perhaps this year we can liven things up a bit. We can't make any firm arrangements until the hospital makes theirs, but let's agree tentatively that we'll get together. You can come to my place if you like. It's a large house, and it's always empty.'

'We must certainly talk it over again,' Mrs Talbot said. 'Marion and I, if she's off duty, rarely see anyone over the holidays, unless we go out. But I prefer the old-fashioned Christmas. Those good old days are gone for good, I'm afraid, but perhaps we can get together and recapture some of the spirit.'

'What do you think about it?' Jim Vincent demanded, glancing at Alan and Marion.

'You go ahead and make any arrangements you like,' Alan said. 'I'm sure they'll suit Marion and I.'

'They will,' Marion concurred with a smile.

'I'm beginning to get that elated feeling which settles on me every year just before Christmas,' Mrs Talbot remarked. 'It must be the true spirit of Christmas. It lasts until the holiday is over.'

'It gives us something to think about during the bleak days of January and February,' Jim Vincent agreed. He glanced at his watch. 'Everyone had enough tea? I think we'd better start back to town now, or we'll be late for this evening's activities. You two youngsters don't mind being on your own this evening, do you?'

'I'll let you know in the morning,' Alan said shrewdly, and Marion felt a surge of happiness as she gazed into his blue eyes.

The drive back to Ambury was pleasant. Darkness was closing in on the car as they set out, and Jim Vincent drove on the way back, with Mrs Talbot beside him in the front. Marion sat with Alan in the back, and before they had travelled very far Alan's hand came out of the darkness and took hold of Marion's. They sat thus until they reached town. Marion was filled with a great feeling of happiness as Jim Vincent brought the car to a halt outside the hotel.

'Well,' he said, turning to gaze at Alan and Marion. 'This is as far as we go together. What about a drink, Alan, while the ladies are preparing for the evening?'

'What are your plans for this evening, Alan?' Marion asked.

'I thought we'd go dancing,' he replied, 'and have dinner later. But if there's anything else you would rather do then say so.'

'No. Dancing will be very pleasant. It's been a long time since I danced.' Marion smiled. 'But I'll have to go over to the home and change. Shall I see you back here in half an hour?'

'That will give us time to have that drink,' Jim Vincent said. 'And what about you, Jessica? Shall we wait for you to change?'

'Oh, no! I can join you later in the bar.'

'That's where I shall look for you,' Marion said as Alan opened the door of the car. 'I shall be a good half hour.'

'That's your privilege,' Alan told her, handing her out to the pavement. 'It doesn't matter how long you take, I shall be waiting. I have waited a long time for this particular evening. But you take your time, Marion. There's pleasure in the anticipation, you know.'

'All right, Alan.' She smiled as her pulses raced. 'But I shan't be long.'

On her walk across the road and into the home, Marion tried to analyze her feelings. But there was no way of putting into clear thought the riot of emotions boiling inside her. She was happy! She was trembling inside with new-found sensations! There were a variety of feelings she never knew existed in her mind. No other man had come close to awakening her as Alan had done. The very sight of him was sufficient to set all her pulses leaping and her heart pounding. She couldn't really believe that it was all happening to her. For months she had seen him around the hospital, feeling the pull of his attraction, slowly finding that her feelings for him were rising above normal standards. But he hadn't been even remotely aware of her existence, until last week, and she was still surprised by his sudden interest.

In her room, which was deserted, for Rebbie had gone out with her latest conquest, Marion wanted to hurry her dressing, to get back to the hotel and into Alan's company but she forced herself to remain calm. She could not hurry, could not show her eagerness. His own rate of progress with her would have to be her guide, although she wanted to throw herself into his arms and declare her raging love for him. She made patience come to her aid, and took a shower before dressing for the evening.

As they were going dancing she chose her pale green dress, and examining her reflection very closely in the mirror. She was more than satisfied with what she saw, and the sight of her dark eyes sparkling made her smile. It was all happening, she told herself. At long last, she had more in her mind than just the thoughts of duty.

By the time she was ready to go back to the hotel she had taken more than the half hour Alan had mentioned, and she picked up her bag and gloves and switched out the light as she left the room. Her footsteps echoed on the concrete paths as she made her way from the home, and she could not help glancing furtively around into the shadows as she recalled Ken Harland's sudden appearance the night before. She sighed with relief when she reached the hospital without incident, and hurried out and across the street to the hotel.

Alan whistled through his teeth when she walked into the bar and he saw her reflection in the mirror. He turned slowly, and Marion was more than satisfied with the admiration gleaming in his blue eyes. He came forward quickly to take her hand, and she imagined he was filled with pride as he walked her back to where his uncle stood.

'You're as pretty as a picture, Marion,' Jim Vincent said enthusiastically. 'I wish I were a young man again, I can tell you.'

'I'm sure you would be a pretty good rival,' Alan retorted with a laugh. 'But you'd better start thinking about your own evening, because after Marion has had a drink we're off. We've done our share of entertaining the old folk today. What would you like to drink, Marion?'

'I'm in the chair,' Jim Vincent replied, and Marion could not keep her happiness from bubbling in her breast as Alan escorted her to a nearby table.

It was some time before Mrs Talbot

arrived, and Marion was watching the door anxiously for her mother. Jim Vincent proved that he was more than ordinarily concerned, because he kept glancing over his shoulder. When Mrs Talbot made her entrance Jim leaped to his feet like a man on his first date, and he hurried away to greet Marion's mother.

'They've certainly made friends very quickly,' Alan said softly, and Marion agreed.

'Perhaps there's something in Vincent and Talbot blood that attracts greatly,' she replied, and Alan nodded his agreement.

'There's certainly a great attraction between us,' he admitted eagerly. 'But now they are together we must be on our way. This evening will go too quickly as it is, and I don't want to waste any more time.'

They waited until Mrs Talbot had been supplied with a drink, and for a few moments Alan made conversation, but Marion could see that he was getting impatient, and she admitted to herself that a certain eagerness was being born inside her.

'Well have a nice time, you two,' Alan said at length, getting to his feet. 'We're off. I don't know what your plans are for the evening, but don't forget to be in fairly early. You're not used to late nights, Jim.'

'I think I could teach you young ones a thing or two,' Jim Vincent replied with a laugh. 'Anyway, don't you worry your heads about us. We shall see you in the morning. I'll leave you to make arrangements for the day out. By the way, Alan, have you made arrangements about your movements this evening? You mentioned earlier that you were on call tonight.'

'Yes, that's all been attended to,' Alan said. 'I'm keeping my fingers crossed tonight. I hope there'll be nothing serious happening around Ambury for a good many hours.'

They took their leave, and Alan was smiling broadly as he helped Marion into his car. When they were driving along the damp streets he glanced at her.

'At last,' he said gently. 'We're out together, and alone. You'll never know how long I've been watching you from afar, as they say.'

'You never gave any sign,' Marion commented. 'I often thought that you didn't know I existed.'

'I've know for a long time, and it was becoming increasingly obvious to me,' he retorted. 'At first I tried to fight it off. You know the reputation I have, and I didn't want to get involved with anyone. I still have a lot to learn, and a great way to go before my ambitions are realized, and I always thought that a woman would add to the burden. But natural feelings can't be suppressed, so here I am out with you, and I'm going to make the most of it, I warn you.'

'I am making no complaints,' Marion said boldly.

They went dancing. Alan took her to a high class club, where they danced before having dinner, and then they watched the cabaret. It was all so new to Marion, who had never made a habit of the social round. Her evenings out before meeting Alan had been a visit to the cinema with Rebbie Norris, or a seat in the local repertory theatre. Now she was like a small child out on her first treat. She seemed to bloom with gaiety, and her spirits communicated themselves to Alan. They danced often, and it was like heaven being in Alan's arms, feeling his hands against her. The music was low and gentle, soothing, setting the right atmosphere for romance, and there was no such thing as time, and reality was far away.

When Alan finally glanced at his watch and sighed, Marion knew a pang of regret. The evening was coming to an end. They left the club and went to the car, and in the darkness of the interior of the vehicle Alan took her into his arms, and this time his mouth found her lips. Marion thrust herself against him, knowing the urgency of passion. At first he was gentle with her, as if unsure of himself, but quickly found his confidence, and he held her tightly, kissing her mouth and cheeks and eyes with a fervour she had not thought possible in him.

'Marion,' he whispered, 'It's been a wonderful evening. What a fool I've been for not asking you out before! I've had the urge to for a long time. Just think! I might have been too late. I know Ken Harland has been getting hot under the collar about you, and I think it was his activities around you that finally pushed me into action. That's one thing I have him to thank for!'

Marion made no reply, and she snuggled up close to him, not wanting the evening to come to an end. But shortly Alan glanced at his watch, and he sighed regretfully.

'I'm afraid time has run out on us,' he remarked. 'I rang the hospital to tell them I would be going home now, so I'd better be on the way in case they try to reach me. You know that emergencies don't wait for any man. But we'll have tomorrow together. That's something to look forward to, Marion.'

'I shall be looking forward to every off-duty period in future,' she retorted.

'And I'll be around to share them all with you,' he said.

They kissed again before he started the engine, and Marion sat huddled in her seat trying to sort out her sentiments as he drove swiftly back towards the hospital. She felt sleepy now, and there was a sense of satisfaction inside her that kept her warm. They were silent until he drew into the car park in front of the hospital.

'I wonder if Jim and your mother had a nice evening,' he commented as he took her once more into his arms. 'They certainly took to each other, Marion.'

'I'm glad for their sakes. I do know that Mother is very lonely, and if she decided after this weekend to sell up in York and move to Ambury perhaps she'll be able to see something of your uncle from time to time.'

'He doesn't live far from here, and

I'm sure he'll do all he can for us and for your mother. He's a very generous man, and nothing is too much trouble for him. I've been like a son to him for as long as I can remember, Marion. I'm glad he's taken to you. But we'll go into that another time. We must walk before we can run.'

His kiss prevented Marion from pursuing the line of thought his last remark evoked in her, and she put her arms around his neck. Now she knew what she had been lacking in her life. Romance was wonderful! It gave her an added sparkle, and the colour that she needed. Nothing seemed to matter now. She was light-hearted and happy. Even the background thoughts of Ken Harland didn't worry her now.

'You'd better run along now, Marion,' he said finally. 'I'd better get to my quarters before they try calling me. I shall see you at the hotel in the morning about ten. Will that suit you?'

'I'll be there early,' she promised. 'What are your plans?'

'A visit to a nearby stately home, and anything else that will keep us in each other's company for as long as possible,' he replied with a smile.

'Thank you, Alan, for everything,' Marion said impulsively. 'I've never had a happier evening.'

'There will be a lot more of them if I have my way,' he replied. 'Would you like me to see you to the home?'

'You'd better not! They don't like male staff around the home after dark.'

'All right. Then I'll see you in the morning.' He leaned across and kissed her gently, 'Goodnight,' he whispered. 'Sleep well!'

'I shall certainly do that after today,' she said. 'Goodnight, Alan.'

She was reluctant to get out of the car, and the cold wind tried to bully her as she stood watching him driving away. Then she sighed contentedly and walked slowly towards the house. She was filled with a magic that would not diminish. Her first evening out with Alan had been an overwhelming success. She

165

couldn't ask for anything more than she had received this evening.

She came down to earth a bit when she walked towards the shadows that lay between the hospital and the home. There had been a lot of talk about lights being put up between the two great buildings, because some of the nurses were nervous of walking through the shadows during the night. Thinking of Ken Harland, Marion clenched her gloved hands as she slowed her pace, and then she took a deep breath and started hurrying. But before she could reach the paths, a tall, heavy figure stepped out of the shrubbery and confronted her, and Marion uttered a brief cry of shock. She knew instantly that this was not Ken Harland. It wasn't his build.

'It's all right, Miss, I'm a police officer,' the man said. 'Don't be alarmed.'

Marion halted with a hand going to her mouth. Alarm swept through her despite his words. What was a policeman doing here? Surely that business of the evening before hadn't induced

Matron to call in the police!

'What's the trouble?' she demanded quickly. 'Why are you here?'

'One of the nurses was attacked earlier,' came the firm reply. 'We aren't taking any chances. There was a similar incident last night. These places are a fascination for certain types of men. But what's your name, Miss? Are you a nurse?'

'I'm Nurse Marion Talbot,' Marion said slowly.

'Then you're the one person Sergeant Snell wants to talk to, came the surprising reply. 'He's in the home at this moment, interviewing all available nurses. I'll walk you through the shadows and see that you get inside safely. But there's nothing to worry about now. The assailant won't be within a couple of miles of the place now.'

Marion was stiff with fear as she walked beside the policeman. A nurse had been attacked this evening! She thought of Ken Harland. But it was ridiculous to imagine that he was responsible. He hadn't attacked her the evening before, despite what Sister West thought about it. But had he been watching for her again this evening, and made a mistake? That was possible, but she didn't think Ken was fool enough to attempt another try for her. She had spoken to him firmly about it, and it was more than his job was worth to go against her wishes a second time.

'Was the nurse hurt?' she demanded. If it had been Ken he wouldn't have harmed anyone. Once realizing his mistake he would have dodged away into the shadows, she was certain. He had made no attempt to harm her the evening before.

'She was almost strangled,' came the shocking reply. 'The man seized her by the throat from behind, and when she resisted he struck her down. She was dazed, but she had enough sense to scream, and keep on screaming. He knotted a piece of string around her neck before making off.'

Marion was horrified by the information, and the coldness in her breast as they entered the home was like ice. Not Ken Harland, she told herself bleakly. He wouldn't have done such a thing! But supposing he had? The thought came unbidden into her mind, and she could not resist it. Supposing he had been drinking again, and decided to do something about his twisted feelings? Had he made a mistake in the shadows and picked the wrong girl? Had he lost his head during the day and decided crazily to do something about the situation which was unfavourable to him? She remembered that he had struck Alan during the previous week, and that showed just how intensely he was feeling about her!

'This way, Nurse,' the policeman said, and opened the door of Home Sister's Office.

Marion entered the office, and a tall, broad shouldered man got up from the desk inside. He stared at Marion with hard eyes as he waited for an introduction.

'Nurse Marion Talbot,' Marion's escort said brusquely, and departed, closing the door of the office behind him.

'Sit down, Nurse,' Sergeant Snell said, introducing himself. 'I must ask you a few questions. I can see you're shocked by the news of the attack that took place here this evening, and I understand that you were subjected to a rather frightening incident last night. Would you tell me all about it, and the name of the man who was responsible?'

Marion sat down, shaking inwardly. Could she name Ken Harland? Perhaps he wasn't responsible for what happened this evening, and if it wasn't then it could only make trouble for him if word of what he had done to her the previous night got out. She sighed deeply as she grappled with her conscience, aware that the sergeant was watching her closely for reaction, and she didn't know what to do. But if Ken was innocent of tonight's attack then he had nothing to worry about.

'Everything you tell me will be treated in the strictest confidence,' the sergeant coaxed. 'What happened to you last night may not be connected with what took place this evening. It is a fact that attempted murder took place tonight, but you were not harmed, so don't be afraid to tell me anything you can. We shall check your story very carefully, and question the man involved. It seems that he is a member of the staff, so his movements tonight can very easily be traced. Now, let's get on with it. You look tired and you're probably ready for bed. I have a lot to do before I can even start thinking of going home. So let's help each other shall we?'

'All right,' Marion said reluctantly. 'But please be discreet in your enquiries. There are always a lot of rumours and gossip around a place like this, and talk can do a doctor's reputation a lot of harm.'

'You can rely on me, Nurse,' Sergeant Snell said, a faint smile hovering around his lips. 'Just tell me in your own words what happened, and any relevant events leading up to last night. I'll do the rest.'

8

Marion spoke slowly as she began to recount the incidents involving Ken Harland that had taken place within the past week, and her voice grew stronger and more certain as she went on. When she had described the happenings on the dark path the previous night she lapsed into silence, and Sergeant Snell nodded slowly. She watched his grim face, but there was no indication upon his features of what was passing through his mind.

'Obviously,' he said at length. 'I must check Harland out, and I'll do it once. Do you know if he was on duty this evening?'

'I'm afraid I can't tell you,' Marion replied. 'I'm on a long weekend myself. I saw him this morning after leaving Matron's office.'

'Yes, I have a report of that,' came the

surprising reply. 'Your Sister West is an amateur detective, it seems. Well I think you can go to bed now, nurse, and forget about all this until the morning. I'll get on with my investigations. I've got one or two leads to work on. I'm certain that your business last night and this mess this evening are the only two incidents that have occurred around here. I've spoken to a dozen nurses already, and none of them has admitted being molested in any way. So perhaps it was a case of mistaken identity this evening. I don't know, but I shall soon find out.'

'You mean that Ken Harland might have been waiting for me tonight, and picked the wrong nurse.'

'I wouldn't like to conjecture at this point,' came the swift reply. 'No doubt you'll be hearing from me again. But there's nothing to worry about. There'll be a plain-clothes man on duty here for the rest of the night.'

Marion left the office and went up to her room, to find Rebbie Norris sitting up in bed, obviously unable to sleep because of the excitement of the evening.

'Marion,' the girl gasped. 'You could have knocked me down with a feather when I heard the news, and I thought immediately that you were the nurse attacked. Have you seen the police?'

'Yes.' Marion sat down upon her bed, feeling weak at the knees. Her thoughts were thrusting up pictures of Ken Harland's face, and she could not forget the intensity which had sounded in his voice that morning when they had spoken together. He had sounded desperate enough to do anything. She shook her head. Rebbie was saying something, and she forced herself to concentrate as she prepared to go to bed.

'Did you tell that smashing sergeant about Ken Harland?' the girl demanded.

'I had to, Rebbie! This is too serious to try and hold anything back. If Ken was after me again then he intended killing me!'

There was horror in Marion's tones, and showing on her face, and Rebbie

Norris sprang out of bed and hurried across the room to her, putting an arm around Marion's shoulders.

'It couldn't have been Harland,' the girl insisted. 'He isn't the type to do anything like that. Your incident with him had nothing to do with what happened tonight. He would have made sure first that it was you he was getting hold of, but this maniac didn't care. He grabbed Nurse Pointer from behind.'

'We'll know in the morning, at any rate,' Marion said, suppressing a shudder. 'But what a terrible business this is.'

They went to bed, and Marion could not sleep for a time. The horror in her mind was too great for her to overcome. A nurse had been severely attacked during the evening, and the knowledge that it might have happened to her, might have been intended for her, made Marion shiver. But eventually she slept, and after spending a restless night she awoke in the morning with a feeling of dread in her mind.

In the nurses' dining hall the talk was about the attack made upon Nurse Pointer, and Marion felt that most of her colleagues were staring at her. No doubt the talk of her own business out in the shadows on the path had got around, and she wondered just what was passing through the minds of these girls. Were they thinking that she had been lucky in escaping so lightly? Had they learned yet that Ken Harland was the man responsible for her incident, and were they thinking that he must have been the man who attacked Nurse Pointer?

'Are you going out, this morning, Marion?' Rebbie Norris demanded, as they were finishing their meal.

'Yes. I'm seeing my mother over at the hotel at ten.'

'I wonder if the police have seen Harland this morning?' the girl pursued. 'He was on duty last night, wasn't he? He could have been prowling around. It looks black for him, Marion.'

'I don't think so,' Marion replied. 'He

didn't harm me the night before. It was just one of those things.'

'You can't be sure of that,' came the swift reply, and Marion experienced a shiver of alarm. She couldn't come to any firm decision in her mind about Ken Harland. Had he been so desperate? There was no way of knowing.

A nurse came into the dining room and bent to speak to some of the nurses at the nearest table. Marion realized that something important had been said because the nurses turned to adjoining tables to pass on what was said, and quickly a ripple ran through the room. Rebbie Norris got up quickly and went to find out what was being said, and she hurried back to Marion as fast as she could move. Marion tensed as she waited for her friend to speak. She didn't doubt that something sensational had happened this morning.

'The police have just arrested Ken Harland,' Rebbie said tremulously. 'That police sergeant took him off to the station.'

'That doesn't prove anything,' Marion said jerkily. Her heart was pounding heavily, and she was breathless. Surely Ken wasn't guilty! She tried to convince herself, but the evidence against Ken was circumstantial, unless he had confessed!

They went back to the nurses' home, and there was excitement in the air as some of the girls congregated and talked about the developments. Marion began to dress for going out, and when she glanced from the window across the paths and shrubbery between the home and the hospital she saw two men at work. One was cutting down the larger bushes and the other was in the first stages of erecting poles. There were coils of electric wire, and a large box of globes nearby, and she knew that the activities of some unknown man had finally persuaded the powers that be to have the lighting installed. But it was too late for Ken Harland, she told herself. If there hadn't been any shadows along the paths he would never have tried to see her, and probably the attack upon Nurse Pointer wouldn't have taken place.

She was almost ready to go out when there was a tap at the door, and Rebbie hurried across the room in answer. Marion turned around as the door was opened, and her heart sank when she saw Sister West standing there, looking towards her with a grim expresion on her heavy face.

'You're wanted by the police, Nurse Talbot,' the Sister said in solemn tones, as if Marion was guilty herself of the attack upon Nurse Pointer. 'There are two men down in Home Sister's office.'

'I'll come right away,' Marion said quickly, picking up her bag. She glanced at her watch. It was almost time for her to go across to the hotel. She followed Sister West along the corridor, and as they were descending the stairs the Sister glanced disapprovingly at her.

'If you had told Matron the whole story yesterday morning perhaps none of this affair last night would have happened, Nurse Talbot.'

'I don't think what happened to me has any connection with what happened to Nurse Pointer,' Marion retorted.

'They arrested Mr Harland on suspicion. Are you still persisting in your statement that it was nothing out of the ordinary what happened to you?'

'I'm sure I don't know anything about it.' Marion closed her lips firmly and refused to say more. When they reached the ground floor she tapped at the Sister's door, and a policeman opened it. He admitted Marion, but refused Sister West permission to enter. Marion went in, finding Sergeant Snell seated at the desk.

'Good morning, Nurse Talbot,' he said briskly. 'I suppose you heard the news about Ken Harland.'

'That he had been arrested?' she demanded.

'Is that the tale going around?' He smiled thinly. 'He isn't under arrest. He's at the station helping us with our enquiries.'

'Do you suspect him of attacking Nurse Pointer?' Marion asked.

'We are suspicious of everyone who had the opportunity to be in that area last night,' came the terse reply. 'But Harland is being most co-operative. He has made a statement covering the incident involving you, and what he says about it tallies largely with what you've said about it. There's no cause for alarm there. He admits that he was too intense when he met you, but he occasioned you no harm, and we're no longer concerned with that. You have no wish to make any kind of a charge against him, have you?'

'Certainly not!'

'That's what I thought.' The sergeant smiled thinly. 'I don't think there's any need for me to detain you longer, Nurse. I hope you'll have a pleasant day.'

'But what about Ken Harland? Did he have the opportunity last night to commit that attack on Nurse Pointer?'

'He denies it, of course, but there is a

chance that he's lying. The attack took place between nine-thirty and nine forty-five. Just fifteen minutes that Mr Harland can't account for with any satisfactory proof. He was in the Wards until a quarter past nine, and he says he went to his room, where he stayed until ten. He has no witness who can bear out his story, so we just have to go on probing and asking questions. In the meantime my men are searching the paths for clues, and if the attacker is a stranger I hope to find something that will prove it, or at least clear Mr Harland. This is a nasty business for an innocent man, especially one in a position such as Mr Harland's.'

'I don't think he is guilty.' Marion spoke firmly, and she believed her own words. 'He's not the type to go around attacking females. What happened between us arose from his feelings. If it had been him last night then he would have known instantly that Nurse Pointer was not me. He would have waited until I showed up, not attack the first nurse who arrived on the scene.'

'That remains to be seen, Nurse. Thank you for your assistance. I'm sure we shall eventually get at the truth.'

Marion turned and departed, and she was thoughtful as she crossed the road to the hotel. Going up to her mother's room, she decided to mention nothing about events at the hospital, and hoped that when he arrived, Alan would feel similarly. There was-no need to alarm her mother.

Mrs Talbot was in very high spirits when she opened the door of her room to Marion, who smiled warmly when she saw how well her mother was looking.

'Do come in, dear. I'm sorry I'm a bit behind this morning, but after such a hectic night I just had to lie in a bit this morning.'

'Did you have a nice time, Mother? Where did you go?'

'We wined and dined extremely well,' Mrs Talbot said, 'And what about you and Alan, dear? Did you enjoy yourselves?'

'Very much so!' Marion wasn't prepared to say too much about it, because she could see that her mother was watching her closely, evidently trying to discover just what relationship existed between Alan and she.

'I think Alan is a very nice person, Marion,' Mrs Talbot observed. 'You'll do very well to keep with him.'

'There you go again, Mother!' Marion smiled gently. 'I have noticed that every chance you get you're on about me getting to know some nice young man.'

'Well you do know one now, so all my breath hasn't been wasted. But now you've overcome you first hurdle I've got to chivvy you on the next. I shan't be satisfied or happy until you're married, my girl.'

'There's plenty of time for that. I'm only twenty-three, Mother.'

'Time you were married, my dear.'

'And how are you getting along with Jim?' Marion changed the subject adroitly. She smiled as her mother launched into the good points she had noticed about Alan's uncle, and they talked generally until there was a tap at the door.

Marion went in answer, and found Jim Vincent standing outside. He greeted her like a long-lost friend, and then his face turned from happiness and pleasure to sorrow.

'I'm afraid I've got some bad news, Marion,' he said. 'Alan just called me. He can't make it today.'

'He can't? But it's his day off! There's no reason why he shouldn't be able to come!'

'I know how you must be feeling,' Jim Vincent said. 'I feel the same myself, and I don't have to tell you about Alan's mood right now. But one of the doctors at the hospital isn't on duty, and Alan has got to take his place.'

'Ken Harland!' Marion sighed. That would be it. Ken was down at the local police station, and someone had to cover for him. It would have to be Alan!

'That's the name Alan mentioned.

Seems that Harland has gotten himself into some scrape or other. I wouldn't have expected it of a responsible person like a hospital doctor.'

'But it can't be helped,' Marion said, stepping back to permit him to enter the room. 'It's knocked the bottom out of our day. Shall we go on as planned?'

'I think we'd better. There's nothing else we can do on a Sunday in December. As a matter of fact Alan suggested that we did just that. He says we can use his car. It will be in the car park across the road. Can you drive, Marion?'

'I do have a licence, but you know what they say about women drivers,' she replied.

'Well you go and pick up his car. If you've got a licence then you'll be able to drive well-enough for me. I'll talk to your mother until you return. If someone saw me taking a doctor's car out of the hospital I'd get taken for attempting to steal it.' He grinned mischievously. 'But that's not the reason why I want you to go. Alan will be waiting at the car if you go right away.'

'I'm on my way,' Marion said quickly, and she smiled at her mother as she left the room.

Alan was sitting in his car when Marion arrived, and she wondered at the seriousness on his face as he greeted her. He must be disappointed about not being able to get out for the day, she told herself as she opened the door and got in beside him.

'I'm dreadfully disappointed about today, Marion,' he said thinly. 'I'm wanted in the Wards now, so I can't stay more than a minute. You know why I'm stuck here today, don't you? It's to do with Ken Harland. Why didn't you tell me what happened the other evening between you two?'

'It was nothing, Alan,' she replied quickly. 'Much more has been made of it than really happened. He didn't assault me at all. I slipped off the path in the dark and lost my shoe and handbag.'

'Well, I don't like it, apart from any other consideration,' he said firmly. 'I'll have a sharp word to say to Harland when I see him.' He gave her a quick, sidelong glance that took in her features. Then he smiled. 'You're looking more beautiful than ever today, Marion,' he said. 'I was really looking forward to today, I can tell you. Do you think Harland attacked Nurse Pointer?'

'I don't think so.' She shook her head. 'It's only circumstantial evidence against him, Alan. What happened the night before has no bearing on last night's incident, but it does make it look black for Ken. I feel sorry for him, myself. If he has fallen in love with me then he's to be pitied.'

'Not if he attacked Nurse Pointer. She's still in bed suffering from shock, and her neck was lacerated by the string which was tied around it.'

'Ken wouldn't have done that,' Marion asserted. 'I'm positive.'

'Evidently the police don't share your confidence in him, or I should be going with you today instead of having to stand by here. Are you going on with the plans? I think you should. Take your mother and Jim on to the stately home and give them a good time. We shall get plenty of time next week to see one another.'

'All right.' Marion smiled gently. 'But it won't be the same without you, Alan.'

'I know. This is going to be the longest day I've ever spent on duty.' He sighed. 'May I kiss you? It will be a consolation for missing everything else.'

She tilted her face towards him, and he slid a hand around her slim shoulders, drawing her gently but firmly into the circle of his arms. Marion closed her eyes, and the power of her emotions surprised her. It was morning, cold and bleak and real, and yet his mouth against hers made her think of dim lights and soft music. She shuddered as a pang stabbed through her. If she needed further proof of the strength of her feelings for him then this was it.

'Kiss me again,' she whispered as he

drew away from her, and he complied quickly.

'Have a nice time today,' he said as he got out of the car. 'You can drive, I suppose?'

'Yes. I can manage quite well. Just explain the gears to me. They are unfamiliar to me.'

Their heads were close together as he showed her the controls, and he kissed her again before closing the door and stepping back from the car. Marion switched on and started driving away, and Alan waved cheerily as she drove out of the park. She went across to the hotel and parked the car, and when she glanced back across the road she could see Alan walking slowly into the hospital through the wide front door.

It wasn't such a happy day as she had anticipated, but Marion hadn't expected anything better after she had learned that Alan could not be with them. However she did her best to put on a cheerful face, out of consideration for her mother and Jim Vincent. They visited the stately home, and stayed most of the afternoon, picnicking in the car for lunch, and Marion thought of the pleasure she would have found had Alan been able to get away from the hospital. But apart from missing him, she was worried about the situation back at the hospital. What had happened to Ken Harland? Was he guilty of that murderous attack upon Nurse Pointer? It was all very worrying, and Marion felt relief when they at last decided to return to town. She drove fast, spurred on by a keen impatience, and did not let up until they had reached the outskirts of Ambury. Her mother was sitting in the back of the car with Jim Vincent, and they had been fairly silent on the return trip. But Jim Vincent came out of his shell when they arrived at the hotel.

'That was a pleasant day, he remarked as they left the car. 'I can understand how you've been feeling, Marion, without Alan with us, and you bore up quite well, attending to us. I appreciate it. Perhaps you'll ring the hospital and find out if Alan will be able to get away tonight. If he can then I suggest I take care of your mother this evening while you go off and enjoy yourself. You deserve it.'

'I don't think he'll be able to get away, Uncle Jim,' Marion said. 'He'll be on duty until tomorrow morning. With Ken Harland not there to take his turn Alan will have to do all of it, and that means being on call as well as standing by.'

'I wouldn't know the difference,' Jim Vincent said. 'But Alan does such an important job in our community that we can't say anything about his being unable to get away. Those poor devils in hospital need his presence a great deal more than we do.'

They went into the hotel, and Marion found that a message had been left for her. It was from Alan, and he wanted her to go across to the hospital to see him as soon as she returned.

'Perhaps he can get away after all,' Jim said. 'Go on, Marion, and find out.

We'll be ready for tea by the time you return.'

Marion agreed, and left the hotel, driving across to the hospital in order to leave Alan's car where she had found it. She went into the hospital and asked at the reception desk for Alan's whereabouts, and learned that he was in the Casualty department. She sighed as she walked along the corridor. She would be on duty in Casualty tomorrow, with the weekend behind her and gone for good, but it didn't matter, because her free time hadn't come up to expectations. Yet she had spent a few happy hours with Alan, and for that she was grateful. He had kissed her, and only a short week before such a possibility hadn't seemed even remotely possible. But all things were possible, she told herself as she pushed through the swing doors. Alan was showing a keen interest in her. He had broken the ice and taken the plunge, and he seemed to like what he found.

For herself, Marion was satisfied.

After a few more outings they would become used to one another, and the sky was the limit as far as she was concerned. The strange feelings fluttering in her breast, like the beating wings of some captive bird, were the beginnings of love. Attraction was giving way before the onslaught of more powerful emotions, and she hoped that the same evolution of feelings was taking place inside Alan. If it was then she could ask for no more.

9

Alan was in the Consulting-room, and he got to his feet with a smile appearing on his face when Marion entered after tapping lightly at the door.

'Marion!' He came towards her with outstretched arms, and she closed the door as she smiled and prepared to slip into his embrace. He kissed her passionately, then stepped back to look at her. 'Did you have a nice time? I've been thinking of you all the while. I've never known a longer or more boring day! But I'm off duty this evening. Norman Howard is going to stand by so I can have a breather. Have you made any plans for this evening?'

'Your uncle has,' she told him with a smile. 'He said that if you could get away he would take care of my mother while we spent some time together. They've both enjoyed themselves today, although they were disappointed that you couldn't be with us.'

Well the best thing to do is forget about today. We'll make up for it later. Have you heard that Ken Harland is still at the police station?'

'No. I haven't heard anything. That does sound bad for him.'

'Officially he's there to help the police with their enquiries, but I think they're afraid he may disappear if they let him go.'

'But they can't hold him indefinitely without making some sort of a charge against him, can they?'

'They can't, and I expect he'll be back here tomorrow. They can't prove anything against him. Nurse Pointer couldn't describe the man who attacked her, and the only thing the police have against Harland is that he can't prove where he was at the time of the attack. He says he was in his room, and they can't prove or disprove it. The thing that makes it really black for him is the business of the night before, when he grabbed you out there on the path. But that must have been a coincidence. Harland isn't the kind of man to do anything violent.'

'But he struck you last week,' Marion said slowly.

'He'd been drinking then. Every man is entitled to make one mistake. If it had been you who was attacked last night then I would agree that he was the most likely suspect, but he wouldn't take it out on someone else. He's a doctor. He's been trained to think in quite different patterns.'

'What time can you get away?' Marion wanted to change the subject.

'At six, which won't be very long. Are you going to wait for me?'

'Have you had tea?'

'Yes. Haven't you?'

'No. I came straight across here when I got your message. I'll go back and have tea, and by that time you should be free to join us.'

'Right.' He kissed her again. 'Are we going out on our own this evening.'

'If you want to.' She smiled into his face, and he shook his head slowly.

'You know something? You're the most beautiful woman in the world. I hope nothing will come along to spoil the friendship that's springing up between us.'

'What could come up?' she wanted to know.

'You might fall in love with some handsome stranger.' He was still smiling, but she had the impression that he was serious.

'I think that's highly unlikely,' she said. 'Don't be too long. I shall be looking for you at the hotel.'

He nodded, and was reluctant to let her go. Marion leaned forward and kissed him on the mouth, and he was so surprised that she was able to slip out of his embrace. She opened the door and moved away, still watching him, smiling, showing in her eyes that she was not lightly flirting with him.

'It will soon be six,' he said. 'I've got an evening all planned out for us.'

'Shall I tell my mother and Jim that you want them along with us?' Marion demanded.

'Don't you dare! Just leave the situation as Jim suggested it. Anyway, I don't think they want to be bothered with us hanging around them. They're quite happy in each other's company.'

'The signs are unmistakable.' Marion paused as she thought about it. 'What do you think about spending Christmas in our company, Alan?'

'I'm praying that a miracle will see us both off duty,' he told her. 'But we'll discuss that later. I've got some more work to do before I can leave here. See you at the hotel.'

Marion nodded and left the department. She went back to the hotel, and found Jim Vincent in her mother's room. They were waiting for Marion, and she sensed that there was an added tension to the atmosphere. But they were both smiling easily, and Marion put it down to her own imagination, which had been working overtime in the past day or so.

'Alan will be off duty at six,' Marion announced.

'Fine. Then you'll be going off with him,' Jim Vincent said quickly. 'I want to talk to your mother, anyway, Marion, and I shall be gone very early in the morning. I have the business to attend to, and I can't stay longer, although I should very much like to.'

'I hope you've had a nice weekend,' Marion said.

'Very nice,' he continued. 'I haven't enjoyed myself so much in a long time. I shall be coming again, and very soon. I'll be writing to Alan about Christmas, and I've made tentative arrangements with your mother. You're coming to spend the holiday at my place, if you can get off duty.'

'I shall look forward to it,' Marion said with a smile. She had taken a liking to Jim Vincent from the very first moment she saw him. 'We'll know very soon just who are the unlucky ones are. I was on duty last year, so I expect I shall be off this year, but one never knows what will crop up in the hospital. The patients come first.'

'Every time,' he agreed. 'But let's go and have some tea. Alan will be over shortly, and we want to be ready for him.'

They went down to the dining room, and Marion found her mother in a strange mood. There was nothing tangible in Mrs Talbot's manner, but something was not quite the same, and Marion found herself wondering what was going on.

After tea Jim Vincent went to pack, and Marion went up to her mother's room. When they were alone she turned to Mrs Talbot.

'Is anything wrong, Mother?' she demanded. 'You seem a little different. You haven't been overdoing it this week-end, have you?'

'No, dear, it isn't that.' Jessica Talbot smiled, and Marion was satisfied. 'We haven't had much time to ourselves this weekend, dear, and I so wanted to talk to you. But I wouldn't have spent the time any other way. However I shall be alone tomorrow, and I'm thinking of returning to York in the morning.'

'I shall be on days next week,' Marion said. 'It would be lonely here for you all day long, but you don't have to go back yet unless you want to.'

'I'm thinking seriously of moving to Ambury.' There was a strange note in Mrs Talbot's voice, and Marion frowned as she studied her mother's expressionless face. 'You would like that, wouldn't you?'

'I'd see much more of you,' Marion admitted, and smiled. 'I wouldn't have to worry so much about you.'

'You could come and live with me instead of staying at the home. It hasn't got the right atmosphere for a young woman. I have been worrying about you, Marion, but now you've got Alan I can have an easy mind. What do you think of his uncle?'

'I like him! Alan is like him a little, don't you think?'

'Yes. I should imagine Alan's father and Jim were almost like twins. Jim has asked me to move here, because York is so far away. He wants to see me, Marion.'

'Well that would be very nice for the both of you, Mother. You're very lonely, and I'm sure he doesn't see much pleasure, always busy with no one to help relieve the monotony. He doesn't live very far from here. It would make a nice day out for you to visit him now and again.'

'I'm glad you agree. That's just how Jim put it.' Mrs Talbot was smiling now, and Marion shook her head as she tried to puzzle out what was passing through her mother's mind. 'In the morning I shall visit an estate agent's and see if I can find a suitable place. If I do I shall go back home and start the wheels in motion. I should be moving within a month, don't you think?'

'You wouldn't want to move before Christmas,' Marion said.

'You're right, but I'll try to be in

Ambury for the New Year. There's nothing like making a change in your life on the first day of the new year.

'You must have doing a lot of thinking on this subject, to be able to make up your mind so quickly,' Marion observed.

'Circumstances made it necessary for a quick decision,' her mother replied. 'Where are you going this evening?'

'I have no idea. Alan said he's got the plans all made. I do feel sorry for him, having to work all day, and he was so looking forward to being with us.'

There was a tap at the door and Mrs Talbot went in answer. Jim Vincent came into the room when the door was opened, and he stared at Marion so hard she could not help noticing.

'Is there a smut on my nose?' she asked with a smile.

'No. I was just telling myself what a fortunate man Alan is. You're very beautiful, Marion. Jessica,' he turned towards Mrs Talbot, who closed the door and came back to where Marion sat, 'you're to be congratulated on having such a lovely daughter.'

'You're a flatterer of women,' Mrs Talbot said with a smile. 'That's the worst kind of man, I was always given to understand.'

'It depends what is behind the flattery,' he replied, and glanced at his watch. 'Alan should be along any moment now. Do you mind if I take your mother out now, Marion? I shall be coming in early tonight because I have to leave on the first train out in the morning. I've asked Alan to bring you over to my place any time you're off duty together. I shall look forward to seeing you, Marion. It isn't more than an hour or so by road, and Alan's got a car.'

'I shall be happy to come,' Marion said. 'I shan't see you again before you leave, so I'll say my goodbyes now. I hope you've enjoyed yourself this weekend.'

'I certainly have! You'll never know just how much,' he replied gently.

'You're a wonderful girl, Marion, and I hope Alan doesn't let you slip through his fingers. He needs someone like you, my dear.'

'Thank you.' Marion was smiling. 'I'm sure we'll come and see you very soon.'

'I'll be able to see you tomorrow sometime, Marion,' Mrs Talbot said, picking up her gloves and handbag.

'Give me a ring in Casualty any time you like,' Marion said.

'I'll do that, and I hope I shall have some good news for you. I know how you've wanted me to move to Ambury. Lock up and give the key in at the desk on your way out, won't you?'

'Yes.' Marion walked to the door with her mother, and again she had the feeling that her mother had something on her mind. But Mrs Talbot seemed happy enough, and Marion saw them off and then closed the door.

A few minutes later there was a tap at the door, and Marion sensed that it was Alan. The door opened as she walked to it, and the next minute she was in Alan's arms.

'I've been waiting all day for this moment,' he said huskily, holding her tightly in his strong arms. 'There seems to be a bad influence working against us.'

'Don't say things like that!' Marion lifted a hand and pressed her fingers against his mouth, and he kissed them tenderly. 'There's nothing against us. I'm sure we've both got a very happy future ahead.'

'Do you read tea-cups, or cards?' he demanded with a smile. 'You're not a witch in disguise, are you?'

'That you must find out for yourself,' she replied, and he nodded eagerly.

'It will be a pleasure,' he said. 'Come on, let's go for a drive. I want you to myself for hours and hours.'

They left the room, and Marion handed in the key at the desk. Getting into the car, Alan caught and kissed her. His face was happy in the light shining from a nearby window.

'They let Ken Harland out of the police station,' he said, and a pang of coldness stabbed through Marion 'He's on duty in Casualty now. Wouldn't let Norman Howard take over. He even apologized to me for having my day messed up.'

'So the police don't believe he's the guilty man!' Marion felt relief sweeping through her. She hadn't thought it was likely, but there had been a large doubt in her mind. She hoped the whole business wouldn't ruin Harland's career.

'It may not be that exactly,' Alan said, starting the car. 'There's no evidence against him.'

'Do you think he did it?' she demanded, and held her breath as she waited for his reply.

'I don't know what to think,' Alan replied slowly. 'I don't like what's happened. He knocked me down and then grabbed you in the shadows. He's certainly worked up emotionally, and he might be the kind of character who blows up under pressure. But if he didn't attack

Nurse Pointer somebody did, and he's a dangerous man to have running round loose. I hope the police will catch him, and pretty soon.'

They drove out of town and Alan parked the car. Marion went quickly into his arms, and they lost all track of time as they sat in the darkness. To Marion it seemed like heaven. She had never felt so happy, and feared that somewhere a setback lay awaiting them. But she wouldn't let anything come between them. They were well suited, and Alan had certainly forgotten that until a week ago he had no interest in women.

When it was time for them to return to the hospital, Alan spoke quietly about the next week.

'I shan't be in Casualty,' he remarked. 'You're going to have Harland. I don't know why they've decided to take him off the wards, but it's probably to do with this business that kept him at the police station all day. Don't let him try anything on with you, Marion. You don't have to put up with it, you know.'

'I think he'll be careful in future,' she responded as he started the car and began turning it. He knows everyone will be watching him. It's going to be hard on him if he isn't guilty of attacking Nurse Pointer.'

'The police won't give up looking for evidence,' Alan assured her, stopping the car again. He stared at her for a moment. 'You know something,' he went on gently. 'I can't really believe that this is true. I've watched you so many times in the past, and I really wanted to talk to you, to try and get to know you, but I had the absurd feeling that you would turn me down flat. You never seemed to speak to a man, let alone encourage one, and I stayed away from you so long because I thought it better to live in hopes than get a flat refusal from you. I can appreciate how poor Harland feels about you. I know I should be upset if you turned me down.'

They kissed, and Marion experienced

a thrill that travelled slowly through her. She was happy that he had finally taken the plunge and asked her out. Her life was complete now, and she knew it. Gone were the dull evenings of remaining in her room, hoping and wondering what it was like to be in love. Now she knew, and she wasn't going to let go of her hold upon romance.

The drive back to the hospital was silent, and when Alan parked in the front of the building Marion stirred herself and looked at him tenderly.

'The weekend is over,' she said regretfully. 'I had been so looking forward to it.'

'There'll be others, and better,' he promised. 'Come along and I'll see you along those paths. We don't want another incident, do we?'

'They were putting up lights, this morning,' she replied. 'It's the same old story of doing things when it's too late. They have been talking for a long time about lighting up that stretch between the hospital and the home.'

'It's a good thing the attack wasn't more serious,' Alan said gravely.

They got out of the car and walked around the hospital, following the paths, and Marion saw that the shadows between the two buildings were gone. A string of lights shone brightly.

'I expect they'll use coloured bulbs during Christmas week,' Alan said with a smile.

'You'll have to make the suggestion,' she told him.

'At the door of the home he left her, and Marion went into the building with some reluctance. All good things had to come to an end, but she was sure that their promise of the weekend would go on, and as she got into bed and switched out the light she was half praying that it would be so. But harsh reality was waiting ahead, she thought grimly, turning to go to sleep. There was a mystery to be solved, and it had to be solved before some other nurse was attacked. She drifted into sleep with thoughts of Ken Harland filling her mind . . .

The next morning was grey, but Marion found her spirits high, and she was smiling as she prepared to go across to the hospital. She went to the dining room with Rebbie Norris, and her friend was quick to notice Marion's joy.

'You must have had a very nice weekend,' the girl said. 'There's a great difference in you, Marion. Has your mother gone back?'

'Not yet. She's going to try and get a house here in Ambury.'

'That will be much better for you, but I shall miss you. There are some nurses on the staff I would positively refuse to share a room with.' Nurse Norris was smiling, and Marion knew the girl was joking. 'I suppose you know you've got Ken Harland in Casualty today?'

'Yes, but what's wrong with that? He's capable.'

'What about it? They have no evidence against him. You don't think he's guilty, do you?'

'Don't you?'

'Not really. He's not the type. Anyway, what harm can he do to anyone in the day-time, and in Casualty?'

'I wouldn't put anything past him after what's happened. I'm glad I don't have to be on Casualty with him.'

Marion smiled as they set out for the hospital, and she left Rebbie at the doorway to Casualty. When she went into the department the first of the out-patients were already seated on the rows of chairs, and Sister West was in the treatment room.

'The doctor isn't down yet, Nurse,' the Sister said. 'Go and check the Consulting-room. I've spoken to the other nurses on duty here today, and I'll tell you what I've already told them. I want you to act as if nothing has happened. Mr Harland hasn't been accused of anything, let alone charged, so let's have no nonsense today.'

Marion nodded and went along the corridor to the Consulting-room. She didn't hold anything against Ken Harland, but she wanted the truth to come out, and sincerely hoped that it would, if only to clear Harland's name. Entering the room, she paused, for Harland was already at his desk, and he looked up from what he was writing and a thin smile touched his lips.

'Good morning, Marion,' he said.

'Good morning,' she said. She paused in the doorway. 'You're not supposed to be here yet. I was going to clean up before you got here.'

'Just forget that I am here, and tell me if I happen to be in the way. I have a lot of paperwork to catch up on. I expect Sister West will be dropping in on me shortly, marshalling the stream of patients to see me.

'She is floating around,' Marion replied with a smile. She studied his face closely as he looked down at the desk. He was looking very tired and strained, and there were dark circles under his eyes. She felt a pang of sympathy for him. All his troubles had stemmed from the fact that he had fallen in love with her, and she could not but think that she was responsible for what had happened. When he looked up again his face was expressionless.

'I'm going to resign my position here,' he said somewhat harshly. 'I'll be gone just after Christmas.'

'I see.' Marion didn't know just what to say. He looked so unhappy that she could not blame him for anything. 'I am sorry about all this trouble that's come to you, Ken. But I'm sure you can see that there was nothing else I could do. If I had encouraged you, or lied to you about anything, then there would have been some justification for your manner, but I didn't do anything.'

'It's all right,' he said steadily, dropping his eyes once more to his work, as if anxious to get back to it. 'But do you believe that I attacked Nurse Pointer?'

'I don't know what to believe,' she

216

replied, and left it at that.

A silence developed, and she began wondering how she could slip away without saying the wrong thing. Then the emergency bell rang, and that was the easiest way out. They both had to go with the ambulance, and they both forgot themselves in the rush to answer the call.

10

The ambulance travelled fast through the traffic, and Marion watched the street outside through the dark windows. She saw Harland checking the treatments bags, and his face was set in grim lines. He seemed to have aged ten years over the weekend, she told herself, and felt sorry for him. But pity wouldn't help him, she knew, and realized that his decision to leave the hospital and go where he was not known was the right one.

'Where's the accident?' she asked suddenly, unable to bear the silence any longer.

'Two lorries have collided on the ring-road,' he replied. 'One of the drivers is in a pretty bad way, and he's trapped in his cab. There's a risk of fire.'

Marion closed her mind to the

pictures which were thrust up by her active imagination. It was bad policy to remember that one was a woman. It was better to cultivate an impersonal manner, to forget all the suffering that was going on inside the patient being tended. Attending road accidents was different to nursing sick people. Sickness was natural, and trying to save the lives of shattered victims at the roadside was not. It took a lot of getting used to, and normally Marion was able to cope, but this morning she felt dithery and realized that despite the pleasantness of the weekend, her nerves had been at full stretch the whole time.

At the scene of the collision there was a great crowd of people from a nearby housing estate, and police were keeping them well back. The fire brigade had been called with cutting gear, and Marion suppressed a shiver as she followed Ken Harland out of the ambulance and across to where one of the two lorries was lying on its side. Glass was scattered all over the road, and a uniformed constable was busy sweeping it away. Firemen were gathered around the cab of the overturned lorry, and Marion compressed her lips as she saw the face of the trapped driver under a mass of tangled metal. A fireman had stripped off his jacket and was lying on the side of the cab, talking to the driver, who had a thin trickle of blood showing on his face. The fireman stepped back as Harland reached them, and for a moment silence settled around them.

'Both his legs are trapped under the engine, which was thrown sideways off its mounting at the impact,' a fireman said, and Marion watched Harland go to work. He climbed up beside the fireman comforting the injured man, and bent to say a few words himself. Marion saw the driver's lips moving slowly, and from where she stood she could see that he was badly shocked.

Harland tried to get close to the injured driver, but the mass of twisted metal that had been the cab prevented him from examining the man. He conversed with the firemen, and work was resumed to cut through the metal. Harland gave the driver a shot of morphine. Then he came to Marion's side. 'He says he's got no feeling in his legs at all,' Harland commented. 'There's nothing we can do until they've cut away some of the wreckage. It's going to be a long wait, I'm afraid, before they finally get him free. But they're working to clear the metal over him so I can see what the damage is. There's some blood on the ground under the cab, so I fear the worst. If that engine has crushed his legs then he'll be in a poor way when we do get to him. He says he thinks he's got some broken ribs, too.'

Marion said nothing. She was shivering with the cold wind blowing through her uniform, and she blamed herself for not picking up her cape. She watched the firemen working desperately to get at the trapped man. The feeling of helplessness that came to her was overpowering.

'Can I get up there where the fireman

is and see if there's anything I can do?' she demanded.

'There's nothing you can do until we get through to him,' Harland retorted. 'He's comfortable enough on the seat inside the cab, and he's unconscious now, so he won't be feeling anything.'

'But he must be nearly freezing in there,' Marion persisted. 'He looks badly shocked. There must be something we can do.'

Harland made no reply, and the two ambulance men came across for instructions. They stood watching the efforts of the firemen to get through the tangle of metal, and there was nothing they could do to help. They would only have been in the way if they had tried to assist the firemen.

It took fifteen minutes to get through what had been the driver's door of the cab, and when the mass of crushed metal had been dragged away the firemen moved back and Marion followed Harland in close. Marion clenched her teeth when she saw the heavy engine lying across the driver's legs, and Harland glanced at her for a moment, his eyes showing what he thought of the situation.

'Ask one of the ambulance men to fetch that other bag over here,' he directed. 'Unless I'm mistaken I'm going to have to take off a leg, or both.'

Marion turned obediently and passed on the message through stiff lips. She went back to Harland's side, and watched him checking the upper part of the driver's body. The wind whistled bleakly around them, but Marion wasn't feeling the cold now. Her thoughts were for the injured man. She threw a blanket over the man's shoulders as Harland turned his attention to the driver's legs, and she crouched at the man's head, one hand resting on his shoulders. He was unconscious, and she was glad of that.

A fireman came close, and Harland consulted with him. Marion listened to their words, and the fireman shook his head as he studied the situation with experienced eyes.

'We've got nothing that will lift it,' the fireman said. 'But there's a garage just down the road. We could send for a breakdown lorry. They could get a chain around it and haul it up enough for us to pull him clear.'

Would you attend to it in a hurry?' Harland demanded. 'I must put tourniquets on both legs. While I'm busy here your men could start cutting through that other side. If the whole top is peeled back the crane will be able to come in directly overhead. We must have a clean lift when it is done. I don't know how badly damaged his legs are, but I fear the worst.

The fireman moved back, and presently his men were sawing at the shattered metal on the other side of the driver. One man went off to the garage, and Marion stood watching helplessly as Harland attended as best he could to the driver's legs. There was a lot of blood on Harland's hands and Marion knew that the situation was becoming desperate. Time was so vital, and time was running out fast for this man.

Then everything seemed to happen at once, and with the arrival of the breakdown lorry they were able to make their preparations. Marion felt nothing but admiration for the firemen and the way they worked. In no time at all the engine was fixed with chains and the firemen were grouped around as best they could, some to steady the engine when it was lifted and the others waiting to take hold of the inert form of the injured driver and lift him out of the wreckage. The ambulance men fetched a stretcher, and Ken Harland crouched very close to the accident victim as the crane winch began to revolve. The big engine shifted a little, and men held it, trying to prevent it from toppling over on top of the driver. Then the crane lifted the weight, and the driver was hurriedly taken clear. They placed him upon the stretcher and he was rushed to the ambulance. Before the vehicle pulled away to start its run to the hospital Harland was busy on the victim's legs, and Marion helped him.

At the hospital an emergency operation was soon under way, and there was no doubt that one of the driver's legs had to be amputated. This was done, and the other limb was cleansed and bandaged. There was hope that it would be saved.

With the operation completed and normal routine taking form again, Marion had time to think about the situation, and she found herself regarding Ken Harland with more ease. He had worked hard for the driver's welfare, and a man who acted like that in an emergency could not be guilty of an attack upon a defenceless woman. The morning was soon over, and Marion went to first dinner. Sister West would be standing by until she returned. There had to be a trained person on duty in case of emergency.

When she returned from lunch and Sister West had taken herself off to the dining room, Marion went along to the

Consulting-room to talk with Harland. She tapped at the door and he called out an invitation for her to enter. When he looked up and saw her standing in the doorway he smiled thinly.

'Not suffering from any ill effects of standing out in the cold for half the morning, are you?' he demanded.

'No,' she replied gently. 'I just wanted to tell you what I thought of the way you acted this morning.'

'You think my humane actions today clears me of that unpleasant business the other night? Is that what you're trying to tell me?'

'I don't know. All I do know is that you must be feeling pretty bad about the whole thing. I am sorry, because what happened between us the night before made it look that much worse for you.'

'You don't have to apologize for telling them what happened between us,' he retorted. 'I didn't attack you, though. We slipped off the path.'

'I didn't mention it in the first place,'

she protested. 'It was obvious that when the attack on Saturday evening took place everyone should think it was you. The talk of what you had done to me on Friday evening was buzzing all over the place.'

'I know you didn't say anything, and for that much I am grateful.' His dark eyes glinted for a moment as he studied her intent face. 'But you don't have to worry about me. I shall be gone within the month. My resignation is expected, anyway, so I am doing the right thing.'

'But it isn't fair if you didn't do anything,' Marion said firmly, and he smiled at her words.

'You're not sure about me, so why should anyone else be? You know what I feel for you, Marion. I love you. Do you honestly think that I would waylay you and attempt to kill you, just because you chose Vincent and not me?' He laughed harshly. 'I'm afraid it's just not on the cards.'

'It's difficult for anyone to believe anything, rightly or wrongly,' Marion said. 'There's no proof one way or the other.'

'That's exactly what the police said,' he retorted, 'and that is why I'm free now. I suppose they'll be watching me, to see if it happens again. It's a wonder they haven't given you police protection.' He laughed and the sound was ugly in the close confines of the office. 'I suppose you had a very nice weekend with Alan Vincent. He doesn't know how lucky he is! You went for him and not me! But I'll bet he doesn't love you as much as I do.'

Marion turned to open the door, and he shook his head.

'I'm sorry if I've embarrassed you, but I'm not ashamed of my feelings. I hope you'll be happy with Vincent, Marion, if he really is the man for you.'

'Thank you, Ken,' she said in a small voice, and left the office. She was convinced now that he was not the attacker. But that didn't relieve the situation at all, because if he had not attacked Nurse Pointer then someone else must have, and that meant a near-maniac was loose in Ambury.

The rest of the afternoon passed away with no call for their emergency service. The Casualty department was busy as always, and by the time Marion got away to tea she was feeling run off her feet. She went to the dining hall, and saw Rebbie Norris seated at a table. Joining her friend, Marion sighed.

'I'm going back until eight,' she said. 'What a day it has been! You're on Men's surgical, aren't you? How is that driver who came in today?'

'On the critical list. You went out to him on the road, didn't you?' Rebbie Norris stared at Marion's face, noting the strain in her friend's features. 'How did you get along with Ken Harland today? He hasn't made any more passes at you, has he?'

'Of course not! And I'm more convinced than ever that he knows nothing about that attack upon Nurse Pointer.'

'The police wouldn't have released him if they'd anything to go on against him,' Rebbie Norris said. 'So we've got a maniac wandering around the hospital after dark. That's very nice for the nurses and the patients, I should think!'

'Are the police keeping an eye on us?' Marion demanded.

'I don't think so. I haven't seen anyone around. It gets dark early these evenings, and it's a long night for the night-staff.'

'We'll just have to hope that they'll catch that man.' Marion tried to sound matter-of-fact, but she knew she didn't fool her friend.

'How can they do that unless he strikes again?' Rebbie demanded. They stared at one another for a moment, reading the alarm in the other's eyes. 'When he does strike again, will it be here at the hospital?' the girl continued. She narrowed her eyes as she stared at Marion. 'And the next time he might kill someone!'

'Don't talk like that,' Marion said

firmly. 'There's no need to spread alarm around. I'm sure the police are as worried as we are, and they're sure to warn their constables to keep a close eye on this place.'

Marion was glad to get away from Rebbie Norris, and she went back to Casualty, busying herself with the work to be done. There were still some people waiting to see the Casualty officer, and going along to the Consulting-room, Marion tapped at the door. When she entered the room she was surprised to see Alan seated at the desk. He looked up at her and grinned.

'Surprised?' he demanded. 'I knew you were working until eight this evening, and Harland had some business to attend to. So I just had to volunteer to fill his place here. I'm off duty officially, but I shall be near you now, although we won't have much time to talk. How many patients are out there?'

'About half a dozen. Do you want to start on them now?'

'Yes, I've been waiting for you to

come back from tea in order to talk to you before becoming immersed in work. Have you seen your mother today?'

'No, I haven't. She said she would call me, but I expect she's been too busy house-hunting.'

'She won't be house-hunting in Ambury, I'm afraid,' Alan said.

'What do you mean?' Alarm speared through Marion.

'Don't worry!' He got to his feet and came to her, smiling broadly. 'I had a good long talk with Uncle Jim on the telephone this afternoon. He told me things that made my ears sing. He proposed to your mother yesterday, and she didn't say no.'

'Alan, you're joking!' Marion stared at him as if she couldn't begin to understand.

'She hasn't said anything to you because she's afraid you might not like the idea.'

'I don't know what to say!' Marion stared at him as he put his hands gently upon her shoulders. 'But come to think of it there was a strange atmosphere in her room at the hotel after I got back last evening from visiting you here. I kept asking her if she was feeling all right. I thought all the excitement might have been bad for her.' She shook her head in disbelief. 'I knew those two had struck up an instant friendship, but this is astonishing.'

'I know exactly how you feel,' Alan said, laughing gently. 'It took the wind out of my sails, I can tell you. But I gave Jim my blessing, and I told him I expected you to do the same with your mother.'

'Of course!' Marion was laughing now. 'But she'll have to wait until I've recovered from the shock of it all. Your Uncle Jim is a fast worker, Alan. You obviously haven't taken after him.'

'Well I like that!' he declared. 'I'm doing all right, aren't I?'

'You are!' Marion laughed easily, and he kissed her quickly.

'Go and let the patients in,' he said

firmly. 'We'll have to look your mother up when you get off duty. We'll surprise her with the news that we know all about her. It seems to me that this last weekend has figured prominently in all our lives. I'm not such a fast worker as my uncle, but you'll have to watch out, Marion. I mean business.'

'I hope you do,' she replied, and her heart was beating fast as she left the office.

The rest of the evening seemed to pass like a dream, and by the time Marion got off duty she had accepted what Alan told her. She was happy for her mother. Loneliness was a curse, and Jim Vincent seemed a very good man. Marion rang the hotel, and was put through to her mother's room. Mrs Talbot spoke normally, and Marion was tempted to blurt out what she knew, but she controlled the impulse.

'Mother,' she said firmly. 'I thought you were going to ring me sometime today?'

'Oh, Marion, I've been so very busy,'

came the swift reply. 'But I knew you would forgive me.'

'Did you go to the estate agent's?' Marion demanded.

'I did, but I haven't settled anything. There are so many details to take into consideration.'

'If you don't want to move here to Ambury then you don't have to just on my account.' Marion was thinking of the situation from her mother's point of view. 'I'm not a child any longer, Mother. You don't have to consider my wants now. Why, you might even think about getting married again. You're still a young woman, aren't you?'

'Married again?' Mrs Talbot's voice rose slightly. 'Why, Marion, where ever did you get such an idea from?'

'Well people do remarry, you know. What about Jim Vincent? He's a very nice person, and he's in the same boat as yourself.'

'Marion, I don't know where you get your ideas from, but you're making me feel uncomfortable.'

'Why I'm not serious, of course, but let's be serious for a moment. You still have your life to lead. If you wanted to get married again then I'd be the first one to congratulate you.'

'Are you coming to see me this evening, dear?' Mrs Talbot quickly changed the subject.

'I've just come off duty. Alan will be finishing shortly, and we'll both come across to see you. Are you going back to York tomorrow?'

'I don't think so, but we'll talk when I see you, dear. Don't be long.'

'I won't.' Marion smiled as she rang off. She handed over to Staff-nurse Jannis, and prepared to go across to the home to change out of her uniform. There were no more out-patients now, and Alan was writing up his reports when Marion looked into his room.

'I'm off now, Alan,' she said, looking around the half open door. 'Shall I come back here for you?'

'Wait a bit and I'll walk you to the home and wait for you,' he said. 'I'm

237

nearly through here, and my relief is on his way down.'

'I shall be all right,' Marion replied. 'Time is getting away. I just spoke to Mother on the phone. She'll be expecting us. By the way, I didn't tell her what you told me. I did skate around it a bit, but she was shy of the subject, so I think it would be better to wait until she's ready to talk about it. Are you sure you got your facts right from Uncle Jim?'

'Yes.' He was smiling. 'Of course they didn't settle anything right away. But it's in the air.'

'I'll be back in fifteen minutes,' Marion said. 'See you then.'

She left the hospital, pulling her cape around her as she felt the tug of the blustery wind. She felt tired. It had been a long day, and her nerves were strained. She wouldn't be sorry to get to bed, she told herself, but she wouldn't miss seeing Alan for any reason in the world.

The paths were lit, and for that she was thankful, recalling the attack upon

Nurse Pointer. The mystery still irritated her mind. She didn't like the way everything seemed to be hanging in the air. Was Ken Harland the guilty man, or had coincidence played a part in the business? Had Ken been after her again on Saturday evening? She didn't like to probe too deeply into the facts. There was only circumstantial evidence against Ken, and she didn't want to judge him. But she wished the police would hurry up and catch the man responsible

Despite the lights she was relieved to get to the home, and hurried up to her room. Entering, she switched on the light and started stripping out of her uniform. Her mind was intent upon other things. She wondered idly if Rebbie had gone out with her boy friend, and there were thoughts of her mother darting around in her brain. She dressed in her two-piece, and pulled on a thick green coat. When she was ready to leave she turned to the door, and found that it was ajar. Frowning, she crossed the room to open it fully, and as she approached she became aware that someone was standing in the doorway, peering through the crack at her.

Marion's heart missed a beat as she paused, and she lifted a hand to her mouth as the door was pushed open. She felt stifled when she saw it was a man standing there, and her eyes opened wide in astonishment when she recognized Ken Harland. Some of her fear fled at sight of him, but she was breathing shallowly, her heart pounding away like a steam hammer.

'Ken,' she gasped, 'what on earth are you doing here? You know this place is out of bounds to you.'

He came into the room and closed the door, leaning his back against it. Marion saw that his face was pale, but he was tense. His eyes showed worry and strain. His hands were shaking.

'I've got to talk to you, Marion,' he said hoarsely. 'It's no use. I can't go on like this. I've tried hard today to forget about you. My brain feels as if it's on fire. What can I do?'

'You'd better get out of here for a start,' Marion said firmly. 'If you're found in these quarters you'd never be able to explain it away. You know you're under suspicion for what happened to Nurse Pointer.'

'You think I did it.' He lurched forward then, and Marion backed away, but he caught her by the elbows, holding her with a strong, desperate grip. She could smell liquor in his breath.

'You're supposed to be on duty,' she pointed out. 'Alan relieved you because you had some business to attend to. Is this your business.'

'I couldn't stay in Casualty any longer,' he said huskily. 'Every time I looked around today there you were. I had to get away. Don't you understand, Marion? I love you. It isn't just infatuation. I can't fight it off any longer. I've been patient, and I've tried everything I know to get you interested in me.'

Marion watched him closely as he spoke, and she didn't like the expression in his eyes. He was near to a nervous breakdown, she surmized, and realized that strains and pressures were aggravating his condition. Now she was not so sure that he hadn't attacked Nurse Pointer, and thinking of what had been done to the nurse, Marion began to feel afraid.

'I keep telling you that Vincent doesn't mean anything,' he went on. 'He's playing around with you, Marion. But I love you. I'd do anything for you.'

'Anything?' she demanded swiftly. 'Would you turn around and get out of here before you're seen? Don't you realize the trouble your presence can cause.'

'Only between you and Vincent,' he said tensely. 'That would be a good thing. If he left you alone you'd have some time for me.'

'Please leave, Ken,' Marion said, trying to keep her voice quiet. 'I am in rather a hurry right now. My mother is waiting for me over at the hotel. She's going back to York tomorrow.'

'You're going to see Vincent. I heard

him talking about it earlier. I hate him! The way he's talking now, anyone would think that you belonged to him.'

Marion felt desperation growing in her mind. He had hold of her elbows, and showed no signs of releasing her. Suddenly she was afraid, and she didn't know why. Instinct was at work inside her, and instinct was never wrong. She realized that she had better humour him, and took a deep breath, hoping that her fear wouldn't sound in her tones.

'Ken, there's still time for us to talk this over. But we can't stay here. If you're seen there'll be trouble for everyone. Go on out the way you came in and I'll see you later.'

'You don't mean that.' He spoke bitterly. 'I can tell by the look on your face that you're only saying it. Once I leave you'll run to Alan Vincent. Well I'm telling you here and now, Marion. Vincent won't have you. If I can't have you then no one will.'

'You're talking foolishly now, Ken,'

Marion soothed. 'Go on, leave and I'll see you outside. You must think of both our reputations, you know.'

His dark eyes seemed unnaturally bright as they stared at Marion, and she felt her spirits sink. He was past humouring! She caught her breath as he turned his head suddenly and struck an attitude of listening. Then she heard it. Someone was coming along the corridor outside, and there were voices. In the silence that followed Marion heard Sister West talking loudly, and while Harland's mind was occupied she suddenly twisted her arms free from his grasp and ran to the door, intent upon getting out into the corridor.

But Harland was too quick for her. She managed to open the door, and she caught a glimpse of Sister West's startled face, and saw Home Sister with her. Then Harland slammed the door and bolted it, and he thrust Marion halfway across the room. She sprawled to the floor, staring up at him as he came swiftly towards her. His face was showing savagery now, and she could not believe that he was the man who tenderly ministered to sick and injured people.

'You shouldn't have done that,' he snarled. 'Now you've gone too far! Come on, get up on your feet and come with me. You think I don't mean what I've been saying, but you'll find out quick enough.'

'Don't be a fool,' Marion gasped as he dragged her to her feet. She heard the sound of someone hammering at the door, and then Sister West was calling loudly.

'Nurse, open this door at once. I know you've got Mr Harland in there with you. Open this door or there will be trouble.'

'We're leaving, but not by the door,' Harland said fiercely. 'Over to the window, and out through it. We'll leave by the fire escape. And don't you make a sound, Marion, or I'll choke you like I did Nurse Pointer!'

Marion stared at him helplesslessly as

he dragged her to the window. So he had attacked Nurse Pointer! The knowledge gave her a sick feeling in the pit of her stomach, and drained away her strength. There was nothing she could do but obey him in the hope that she might be able to give him the slip later. But she was trembling uncontrollably as she climbed out through the window, swaying on the iron fire-escape in the blustery wind. There was a narrow balcony running along the length of the building, connecting all rooms by their windows to the ladders leading to the ground. The floors were connected by ladders at the corners of the building, and when Marion reached the nearest corner and started to descend, Harland seized hold of her and jerked her away.

'We're going up, not down,' he said ominously. 'They won't think of looking for us on the roof.'

'Please,' Marion said desperately. 'Stop this before you go too far, Ken. I'm sure we can explain it all if we get to Sister

West before she makes a report.'

'Shut up and start climbing. We're going up on the roof.' There was menace and determination in his voice, and Marion felt a twinge of alarm. She was despairing of breaking away from him, and that thought had occupied her mind from the moment he had started using force. But now she wondered what he had in mind, and as she climbed the slippery iron ladder towards the roof, her heart almost failed her. Was he going to harm her, as he had tried to harm Nurse Pointer?

11

When she reached the roof, Marion looked around wildly. In the darkness this place was unrecognizable as the spot where most of the nurses sunbathed in the Summer. Now rain was slanting down, and the cold wind threatened to lift Marion bodily and hurl her over the side of the tall building. She felt Harland's hand come out of the darkness and grasp her arm.

'Come on,' he shouted in her ear. 'Let's get in the shelter of that building over there.'

'What's on your mind, Ken?' she demanded in shrill tones. 'There's no sense to this.'

Her words were torn from her lips by the wind and hurled away into the darkness. Rain spattered into their faces as he pulled her towards the dark mass of the low building. He made no reply, and when they stood in the comparative shelter of the building Marion gasped for breath.

'The cat is out of the bag,' he said loudly. 'They'll guess what I'm up to when they find your room empty. I told you that I attacked Nurse Pointer, didn't I?' He laughed harshly, and there was a cracked note in his tomes. 'I heard her earlier that day talking about you and Vincent, and she said some very unkind things about me. She never even apologized when she saw that I overheard. People are cruel, Marion, and you've been worse than any of the others. I love you more than anything. I can't bear the thought of living without you. I won't have a moment's peace, thinking about you with Vincent.'

'What about Nurse Pointer?' Marion demanded.

'I was waiting for you to turn up. I knew you were out with Vincent, and I was in a filthy mood. When I recognized Pointer I thought I'd teach her a lesson. It started off as a sort of a joke, really, and then it got out of hand. When I got hold of her I lost all sense of reason, and started strangling her! Well that taught her a lesson. She won't be able to talk for a few days yet.'

'Why didn't you admit to it and tell the police what really happened?' Marion demanded. 'There wouldn't have been much fuss made about it. But you tied string around her neck, Ken. What were you thinking about?'

'Who gives a damn what I think.' He kept a tight hold on Marion's arm, and his fingers dug into her soft flesh. 'What am I going to do now? I'm in a real mess.'

'There's only one thing to do. Let's get down from here. We can do it from the inside. There's a flight of stairs inside this building.'

'There is?' He stiffened, and seized her with his other hand. 'Why didn't you say so before? The police will be here before long, and they'll be able to come at me from all sides. What can I do?' He looked around wildly in the night, and Marion felt a tremor of fear rising inside her. In his present state of mind he might be capable of anything. It was obvious to her that the pressures within his mind had upset the equilibrium of his reasoning processes, and possibly his sanity. His actions now were definitely unreasonable. She knew she could not afford to aggravate him, and if she could she had to talk him into going down to the ground.

'Ken, you can get out of this quite easily,' she said, trying to keep her tones steady and matter-of-fact. 'Look, if we get down from here before Sister West sends for the police we can both deny that we were ever in my room together. If they don't catch you redhanded there is nothing the police can do about it. You realize that from the fact that they can't arrest you for attacking Nurse Pointer.'

'But you know about it now, and you're not the sort to keep quiet about it. You'll report it, Marion. If you were in love with me you might consider covering up for me, but you're in love with Vincent, and that puts me out in the cold.'

'So what are you going to do? If the police come they'll search everywhere, and they'll find you up here with me. What will you do, Ken?'

Marion had to ask the question. She couldn't stand the strain of wondering what he might do. If he was temporarily unbalanced he would be capable of anything, and she dreaded some of the thoughts that her imagination fired so briskly in her mind.

'I don't want to go on living,' he said calmly. 'If they come up here I think I'll jump off the edge.'

It was like a nightmare, but it seemed so unreal because he was not acting like a raving lunatic. Marion was silent for a moment, stunned by his words. Surely he didn't mean it! He must be playing some kind of macabre joke! But she couldn't forget that he had half-strangled Nurse Pointer. That hadn't been a joke.

'And what about me?' she demanded, with a quiver of fear in her tones.

'I'll take you with me.' He spoke fiercely, turning towards her, grasping her wrists and pulling her close to him. She could feel the heat of his breath against her cheeks, and the smell of whisky was strong in her nostrils. 'If I can't have you then Vincent won't.'

'Don't be a fool!' she panted, struggling vainly to break his grip. 'You're a doctor, Ken, a responsible person. You don't have to act like a crazy, teenaged roughneck.'

'You'll see,' he promised, and kissed her.

Marion tried to fight him off but her strength was gone. Fear had weakened her from the moment he had forced her to climb out through the window of her room. The unreality of it all had a great effect upon her. She thought of Alan awaiting her return in Casualty, and of her mother in the hotel across the street. Surely this was just a bad dream!

'Let's go down from here, Ken,' she

said urgently. 'I'm cold.'

'We'll stay here.' He shook her roughly, and Marion's spirits sank still lower. 'You think I'm playing some kind of a game?' He broke off then and turned his head away, listening intently, and hope flared in Marion's breast.

What would Sister West have done? Knowing her superior, Marion realized that the Sister would have raised the alarm immediately. The police would be on their way now, she felt a spark of comfort as she pressed herself away from Harland. But she could not break his grip. He was like a giant against her, and she couldn't help thinking that she must be dreaming, and that very soon she would awaken and find it so.

'Ken, listen to reason, she pleaded. 'If the police come they'll surround this place, and you won't be able to get away. Go now, before they catch you. Leave me here. I shan't raise the alarm.'

'Let them come. There's nowhere I can run to. But they won't take you from me.' He released one hand and reached into his pocket. When his hand appeared again there was a glinting object gripped in it.

'What's that?' she demanded.

'A scalpel!' He laughed ominously. 'I'll kill you, Marion, and then myself. I can't face this situation any longer. There's no way back for either of us.'

Marion was frozen with fear, and she could not take her eyes off the glinting weapon in his hand. It was a familiar object, an everyday instrument that she handled or cleaned, and one which he was skilled in using. But he had never used it for a savage purpose. She tried to appeal to his instincts as a doctor.

'Ken, put that away. You wouldn't insult your profession by even talking about such wicked things. This has gone on long enough. Let's go down now.'

'Be quiet!' He was peering into the darkness again, and Marion felt a desperate ray of hope. — Were the police here already? Had they started closing in on the rooftop?

'Ken, I'm freezing,' she declared. 'It's been a long day. Let's go down.'

'Shut up.' His tones were high pitched, and Marion recognized the sound. She shivered, and not from the cold, as she subsided. 'There's someone over there. I heard a sound.'

'It's the wind,' Marion told him. 'They won't think of looking for us up here. They'll think we were afraid of being faced with the knowledge that we were seen together in my room. They'll think we've gone into town.'

'I don't think so. Sister West is no fool. Listen. Can't you hear that? Footsteps on the ladder leading to the roof. It's unmistakeable.'

There was a trembling inside Marion that threatened to overwhelm her, fill her with panic and betray her to his twisted ways. She knew she had to keep talking naturally in order to hold his attention. He was trying to goad himself into some rash act, and with that scalpel in his hand there was no limit to what damage he might inflict upon her.

'Ken, you're not such a bad person! I do have a lot of feeling for you. But you were pestering me with your attentions. But for that I might have gone out with you.'

'It's too late to start talking like that,' he said slowly. 'I know what you're up to, but it's no use.'

He moved quickly then, spinning her away from the shelter of the side of the building, and Marion caught her breath, fearful that her last moment had come. He kept hold of her hand, pulling her as he started running, and Marion turned her head, wondering what had startled him into action. She felt a wild surging of hope when she saw several dark figures rushing after them. The police!

It had to be! And they had come up to the roof by way of the inside stairs. There were shouts of warning from behind, and Marion turned to look at Harland, although it was too dark to see his features. He was dragging her along, and with a start of horror Marion realized that he was making for the edge of the building. He planned to jump off, taking her with him.

Marion screamed, and saw Harland's face turn her way. He was still holding the scalpel, but he made no attempt to touch her with it. His face was just a grey blur in the night, but there was a glint to his eyes and teeth. His breathing was heavy, sounding harsh in the wind, and Marion tried to set her heels in on the slippery roof, hoping against desperate hope that she could stop him, or even slow him enough for the men at their backs to catch them.

'Come on!' Harland cried, and he paused in his stride and turned towards her, threatening her with the scalpel. Marion screamed again, and threw herself backwards, falling heavily upon the roof. Her surging weight broke his hold upon her arm, and he went several feet under his own momentum. Then he turned and came back, and Marion screamed again when she caught sight of the glinting scalpel in his hand. The keen blade was sweeping in to connect with her flesh.

But she saw a figure rising up from behind him. Someone was climbing the last few feet of the fire-escape ladder. Marion caught her breath, frozen now, paralysed by the fear inside her. She saw Harland pause in the act of slashing at her, and knew that he must have heard the sound of desperate feet on the ladder. He looked around, and now the figure at his back was almost within arm's length. Harland cried out in anger, whirling quickly to face the danger, and Marion's breath caught in her throat when she recognized the figure closing with the dangerous man. It was Alan!

It was like watching a film, but no film had ever held her so spellbound! Harland lurched forward, recognizing Alan, and the healing knife in his hand was intended for swift murder. Marion saw the glinting weapon swing towards Alan, caught her breath as he ducked quickly, and then Harland was flying over Alan's head.

For a moment the action seemed suspended. Alan was poised to turn and face Harland, who was in the air. Then Harland hit the roof with a thud, sprawling on his hands and knees, trying desperately to get upright, and he was in the act of straightening when his momentum took him to the edge of the roof. There was a low wall between him and a long drop to the ground, but he was off balance, and there were no holds for his desperately flailing arms. Marion heard a sudden trailing shriek of terror that the wind could not tear way, and then the sight of Harland's twisting figure disappeared quickly. The sound of the shriek seemed to go on and on in her mind.

'Marion!' Alan was bending over her, reaching out tender hands to take hold of her and raise her from the wet roof. Other figures suddenly appeared, and she recognized the voice of Sergeant Snell. But it was Alan who held her attention. She was trying to fight off the terror that tried to seize her mind. Now the drama was done reaction was spilling over, shocking her badly. But Alan put his arms around her and held her close, unmindful of her wet clothes. 'Are you all right, darling?' he demanded. 'I nearly went crazy when I heard what had happened.'

'I'm all right,' she whispered. 'But I'll never want to come on this roof again.'

'Take her down,' the police sergeant ordered. 'I'll have to take a statement later, but I think I have all the facts now.'

Marion heard his voice as if he was moving away from her all the time. It grew fainter and fainter, and then she realized that she was crumpling. It would be silly to faint, she thought remotely, and felt Alan's arms take her bodily and lift her up. As she lost her senses she was aware only of the comfort of being in Alan's arms, and she knew that when she awakened again the nightmare would be over. With that knowledge she felt free to release her frantic hold upon reality, and she was almost happy as everything blacked out. Alan was here, and he would always be here in the future when she needed him!

We do hope that you have enjoyed reading this large print book.

Did you know that all of our titles are available for purchase?

We publish a wide range of high quality large print books including:
Romances, Mysteries, Classics
General Fiction
Non Fiction and Westerns

Special interest titles available in large print are:
The Little Oxford Dictionary
Music Book, Song Book
Hymn Book, Service Book

Also available from us courtesy of Oxford University Press:
Young Readers' Dictionary
(large print edition)
Young Readers' Thesaurus
(large print edition)

For further information or a free brochure, please contact us at:
Ulverscroft Large Print Books Ltd.,
The Green, Bradgate Road, Anstey,
Leicester, LE7 7FU, England.
Tel: (00 44) 0116 236 4325
Fax: (00 44) 0116 234 0205

Other titles in the
Linford Romance Library:

THE RIGHT MR WRONG

Pat Posner

When Tiphanie tells her boyfriend Howard she'll have to cancel their holiday to go and help her brother look after their niece and nephew, the consequences are catastrophic. Reeling from the breakup, Tiphanie arrives at her brother's home in a beautiful area close to the salt marshes, anticipating just a little peace and quiet. But any such hopes are dashed thanks to inconvenient feline escapades, a couple of very lively children, and her rather irksome — yet gorgeous — neighbour Kyle . . .

FINDING THEIR WAY

Angela Britnell

Attempting to shake off writer's block, novelist Fran Miller comes to the Cornish village of Tresidder to spend the summer with her long-time best friend, Lucy. She definitely isn't looking for romance, especially after a painful breakup with her last boyfriend — but it finds her nevertheless in the form of Charlie Boscawen, local baker and heartthrob. Soon she is being wooed with the most tempting confections imaginable. But Charlie has problems of his own ... and what will happen when the summer comes to an end?

FINDING ALICE

Sarah Purdue

Evie Spencer has always lived life cautiously, wary of trusting anyone other than her beloved younger sister Alice, a talented painter who is studying art in Rome. Then Alice suddenly disappears — and Evie, determined to find her, must throw caution to the winds. Inexplicably stymied by the British Embassy, Evie is frustrated and desperate . . . until the mysterious Tom De Santis offers assistance. But there is more to him than meets the eye. Can Evie trust him, and succeed in finding Alice?